APOSTLE

APOSTLE

DAMIAN'S CHRONICLES™ BOOK THREE

MICHAEL TODD   MICHAEL ANDERLE
LAURIE STARKEY

LMBPN

DISRUPTIVE IMAGINATION

LMBPN Publishing
PMB 196, 2540 South Maryland Pkwy
Las Vegas, NV 89109

First US edition, November 2018

DEDICATION

To Family, Friends and
Those Who Love
to Read.
May We All Enjoy Grace
to Live the Life We Are
Called.

PROLOGUE... TEN YEARS BEFORE

The gravel crunched under Damian's boots as he walked carefully behind Calvin. He ducked, and a branch whipped over his head. The team moved toward their target, a run-down amusement park from the fifties, far off the beaten path.

Korbin put his hand up to slow the crew as they turned the corner. Large wrought-iron gates were rusted in their tracks. Johann's long blond ponytail slipped off his shoulder as he nodded at Mary. She clutched her med bag and drew her gun.

Calvin joined them and crouched behind the bushes to the left of the gate to peer through the metal rails. "This place is fucking creepy."

Damian chuckled and focused his binoculars. "Apparently, it was the place to be on a Friday night out here."

"Looks like the place *not* to be now." Calvin wrinkled his nose at the derelict buildings and trash scattered around. "And look where I am, spending Friday night with the fucking carnies."

Johann grasped two bars and stared between them. "It's derelict now, but why did they close it? In its heyday it would have been awesome."

Mary smirked. "You thinking of investing in some property, Jo?"

Johann shrugged. "Yeah, but more like a hut on the beach than Nightmare Central."

Korbin chuckled. "In 1963, the place was hopping. They installed new rides, new lights, and modernized it. Then, in November of that year on this very date, the morning maintenance crew found a body. A girl had been strung up on the Ferris wheel, and there were obvious signs of demonic ritual sacrifice. Management announced the closure of the location—something to do with the land rights, but that was clearly bullshit."

"Nothing like a good ol' demon sacrifice to ruin the damn party," Damian said grumpily. "Seriously, they should have cleaned up and kept going. When we close shit down, we tell the demons that they won."

Calvin inhaled deeply through his nose and glanced at the priest. "You gotta understand the fear a demonic sacrifice put into them. God-fearing folk don't want to play where demons hang out."

"That's right." Korbin nodded and drew his gun. "The rumors had already spread. The only way they could hide the whole truth was because the girl wasn't from the town or even the state. The owners would have spent more money fighting the rumors than they lost shutting down. I think they were freaked, too. They abandoned everything, and didn't even dismantle it. The family still owns the property, but they don't come here."

Mary stretched her neck to ease the tension. "Let's get this show on the road. I don't need any freaky carnies coming out of the woodwork. I'll crawl through the bushes and see how many guards are at the front gate."

Damian put his bible in his jacket pocket and climbed the fence. "I'll check the park out from up there. Be right back."

Korbin glanced at Calvin, who raised an eyebrow. "What? Hell, no. My black ass is staying right here on the ground. I'll work when we get inside."

The team leader laughed and nodded. "Sounds good."

Mary and Damian finished their respective reconnaissance and returned. The priest hopped off the fence and brushed twigs from his jacket. "There is a building to the right and directly inside the gate with two gun-toting Damned pacing the roof."

Mary nodded, breathing heavily. "There are two demons at the front gate and another pair about a hundred yards down at a service entrance."

Korbin nodded and rubbed his hands together as they huddled. "Damian and Calvin, take the front gate. Mary and Johann, clear the service entrance. I'll move to the gravel road and snipe the two on the roof."

The team nodded agreement and readied their weapons. Their leader sprinted along the tree line, waiting for Damian and Calvin to make their move. The latter drew his gun and glanced at his teammate. "You exorcising?"

The priest grabbed his bible in one hand and his pistol in the other. "You know it."

They moved furtively forward. Calvin stepped to the side and Damian rushed the first target. He grabbed it by the neck, slammed it to the ground, and held the bible in its face. He'd started a prayer but quickly saw that there was no human left inside. The demon had taken the soul, and the body was simply a husk.

He punched the beast in the face with his bible and growled with irritation as he shoved the book into his pocket. Flipping his gun to his right hand, he stood and aimed, giving Calvin the signal. He pulled the trigger twice as his partner ran past, already firing at the other guard. With both targets eliminated, the fighters glanced at the service entrance, where Mary laughed loudly.

She straddled one of the demons and maintained a choke-hold. "You like that, asshole? You demons are into that kinky shit, aren't you?" She pulled the trigger. "Is *that* kinky enough for you?"

The creature turned to dust, and she glanced at Johann. He just shook his head, and she shrugged. "What?"

Her teammate rolled his eyes. "So dramatic."

Two shots rang out from the road, and the guards on the roof dropped. The team watched as Korbin jumped to his feet. Mary slapped Johann on the chest. "*That's* what I'm talking about. Pure talent."

The team leader met the others at the service entrance and knelt to spread a map on the ground. He checked the number over the service entrance and pointed to its location. "We're here. The main area amphitheater is through this service entrance, down about halfway, and out to the left. We should see the main area from there. I don't know what we'll walk into here, lock and load."

The team huffed in unison, a silent battle cry. Korbin took the lead and walked slowly through the entrance with his gun ready. Johann and Mary fell in behind him to watch their flanks, and Calvin and Damian brought up the rear. The service hallway was silent, and lights flickered from an entryway ahead. Korbin put his finger to his lips, and the group huddled against the green tarp that separated the spaces. They inched to the opening and poked their heads around cautiously.

Mary gasped quietly, and Johann shut his eyes and stepped back. Damian pushed forward and peered over Korbin's shoulder. Four crosses on the stage each held an older person dressed in worn staff maintenance uniforms. The bodies were nailed in place, their entrails spilled. They were obviously dead.

Korbin pushed the priest back and swallowed hard. "Okay. There are eight demons in that main area. We're obviously too late for the people. Still, these monsters need to be stopped. Damian, do your thing. Save as many as you can. The rest of you, stay alive and eliminate the rest. Mary and Johann, take those three on the right. Damian and Calvin, those three on the left. I'll handle the two onstage."

The group surged into the main area. The priest curled his lip at the foul stench of demon and old blood. The bodies weren't fresh. He grabbed a demon by its throat and slammed the butt of his gun into its head and launched into an exorcism prayer. *"Domine tolle istorum simulatione fallatur. Deiice illos..."*

He exorcised the two demons he could and laid the

human bodies gently on the ground. The rest, though, were too far gone. The team dealt with them quickly and easily and watched Korbin battle the last beast onstage.

Calvin chuckled as the fighter roundhouse-kicked his adversary's chest. "I swear the dude never ages. He's like fucking Chuck Norris."

Damian holstered his gun as Korbin decapitated his opponent. "I was waiting for one of them to slip on a liver or something."

Calvin tried to stifle his laugh. "Bro, that's...too soon, dude. Go tend to your sheep."

The priest smirked as he moved to the two young men passed out in the dirt. He checked each pulse and nodded to Mary. "They should be fine. We'll load them before we go, but do me a favor and check their vitals one last time."

She gave a thumbs-up. "Might as well practice my medic duties on someone. You boys keep it clean out here."

Johann walked past. "Complaining?"

Mary chuckled. "Nope, observing. You could at least get a fucking papercut every now and then."

Damian walked away from the conversation and studied the stage. The corpses on the crosses didn't make much sense to him. The amusement park had a reputation for child sacrifices, not adult.

Calvin joined him and folded his arms. "It's a damn shame."

Damian nodded, and his gaze shifted into the distance as he strained to listen. "Do you hear that?"

The other man listened closely, then nodded. Music played faintly from the shadows. The priest frowned.

"Sounds like a music box." He headed immediately toward the sound, drawing his pistol.

Calvin groaned and hurried beside him. "Dude, this is stuff you don't chase down. I'm serious."

They headed between the wrecked rides and past the crumbling game booths. Damian's gaze roamed the scene quickly, looking for any sign of demons. The music ended abruptly, and the men halted, looking around. Calvin shuddered, staring at a torn picture of a clown hanging on a post by one corner. "Where did it go?"

Damian was about to respond when a deep, eerie chortle sounded from their left. The priest turned quickly, his pistol ready, and studied the old funhouse. Calvin tilted his head back and tightened his grip on his weapon. "Come on, man. Are we really going in there?"

"Hey, who says you can't continue the fun of Halloween into November? Come on. Let's check it out."

They inched their way into the structure, noting the striped wallpaper peeling in ragged strips. They stepped into a room full of old mirrors, and Calvin turned his flashlight on. As they crept forward, he gasped and fired a round instinctively into a reflection. He turned quickly to catch a demon's arm before its claws raked his body.

Calvin wrestled with his attacker and crashed into one of the mirrors. His gun fell from his hand, and he snatched a glass shard, grimacing at the flesh melting from the fiend's face. "Fucking creepy."

He stabbed the demon's throat, almost severing its head. The creature squealed and turned to ash.

Behind him, Damian cleared his throat. "You done playing around?"

The fighter scoffed and stood. He brushed remnants of glass from the front of his pants and retrieved his gun. "I'm about ready to get the fuck out of here."

The chortle sounded again, and they raced through the next door into an area where the walls slanted and a central platform shifted continuously from right to left and back. An old, dirty clown sat on the moving dais with his back to them. His costume was riddled with holes and covered in small, bloody handprints.

Damian raised his eyebrows. "Fuck. Hey! What are you doing, Bozo?"

The demon's laughter ceased, and it turned slowly to reveal a disfigured, painted clown face. The beast roared, and rows of sharp teeth dripped with saliva. The priest's gaze shifted and settled suddenly on the faces of five children sitting cross-legged on the floor. Their eyes all glowed bright red.

Immediately, the fighters raced toward the clown. Calvin caught the creature in a choke-hold. Damian held his bible up for a moment but dropped it at his feet. The demon bucked free, and Calvin fell against the side of the room. He grabbed his pistol, but the enemy struck it from his hand. Stepping back, Damian tripped and fell off the platform. His hand grazed his bible as he prepared for the inevitable. The fiend raised his claws high, ready to strike, but two shots rang out.

The priest opened one eye and stared at the bullet holes in their adversary's forehead. The beast screeched loudly and burst into a cloud of dust. The two men glanced at Korbin who had entered ahead of Mary and Johann. His smoking gun barrel told the story. Damian nodded in thanks and ran to the children. With his bible held gently in front of them, he began the exorcism prayer.

The words spilled from his mouth, but he could tell the demons were too strong for their tiny little host bodies. They ripped the children apart with every word.

Calvin walked up, knelt beside him, and put his hand on the open bible. "Brother, they're too far gone. I'll take care of this one."

Damian shook his head, his gaze fixed on the bouncing blonde curls of a small girl. "No. No, they can't be gone. *No.*"

Korbin grabbed the priest's arms from behind and hauled him to his feet. He grabbed his shoulders and turned him away from the children. "Damian! Let it go. Come on."

He stared at the team leader for a moment, tears welling in his eyes. Unable to speak, he followed Korbin as Mary and Johann joined Calvin on the platform. He stepped through the doorway and recoiled involuntarily when several gunshots echoed through the funhouse and his soul. Against his better judgment, he glanced into the room. A small hand peeked from behind the platform, stained with blood.

He closed his eyes and drew a harsh breath. That fight had changed him forever.

CHAPTER ONE

Thunder crackled across the London sky, and lightning lit up the living room where Damian sat clutching his book. The fire shimmered as a breeze gusted down the chimney. His gaze locked on the front door and he wondered if he had imagined it. Slowly, he closed his book and scooted closer to the edge of the chair. He hadn't actually heard a knock, surely. It was only the wind playing tricks.

As his shoulders began to relax, thunder rumbled again, and the front door shook with another pounding demand. Damian swallowed hard. He hadn't imagined it. There actually was someone at the front door that late at night.

Ravi hissed. *I don't like this. I can't sense if there is something out there you should worry about.*

The priest set the book on the table. *What choice do I have but to open it?*

The demon chuckled nervously. *Uh, how about you don't go to the door? Whoever it is will think you are asleep or not* home and go away. *Maybe they'll come back at a more appropriate time, like daylight.*

Damian shook his head. *Whoever is here obviously thinks it's important. I can't not answer it.*

She huffed, using her strength to immobilize him. *Hear me out. You are in here, your guns are out there, and you slay fucking demons for a living. That could be some badass demon, ready to mow you down as soon as you open the fucking front door. Seriously, think about this.*

He grunted and tried to free himself. *I am thinking about it. And let me ask you this: since when do bloodthirsty, angry demons knock politely? Don't you think one of those would be in here already?*

Ravi was silent for a moment. *True, but it could be a new tactic.*

Damian rolled his eyes, and she released her hold. *Yes, because manners are high on their list of war tactics. Take a deep breath, Ravi. We will be fine. I wouldn't take risks unless I truly believed I had to.*

He stood and walked quietly to the entrance, placing his steps to avoid making the worn floorboards creak. At the door, he leaned forward to the peephole. A porch light shined behind the visitor, shadowing their face. From the silhouette, he assumed it was a man, but the peephole wasn't large enough for him to see much. Whoever it was, they either weren't infected or had masked the red in their eyes. That couldn't be mistaken, even in the dark.

Ravi whispered, *Who is it?*

Damian straightened. *I don't know. I can't see their face, but I don't think it's a demon. I don't see red eyes.*

Just then, the person pounded again, and the metal

door handle rattled. Damian shook his head at his nerves. He grasped the lock with one hand and the handle with the other, closed his eyes, and said a quick prayer for safety. After a deep breath, he yanked the door wide and immediately assumed a defensive stance. He narrowed his eyes as the person lifted their head.

"Wally! Good Lord, man, what are you doing here? And at this hour?"

His friend looked like he hadn't slept in days. Water poured over his wide-brimmed hat, and his clothes were utterly soaked. Large dark bags shadowed his eyes, and his lip twitched nervously as he peered over his shoulder. It was obvious that Wally had something serious on his mind.

The priest shook his head and pulled the man inside. He shut and locked the door behind him, pulled a towel from the nearby closet, and handed it to his friend. Wally rubbed his face and removed his hat. Damian hung his hat and coat on the rack and waited for the visitor to collect himself.

His hands were white and shaking, and his face seemed frozen. He frowned, and his gaze shifted nervously to the fire. In silence, he relinquished the towel and allowed his host to lead him to the blaze.

Damian watched quietly as Wally extended his hands to the warmth. Finally, when a little color had returned to his cheeks, he said, "I'm so sorry for coming here without calling. I know it's terribly late, but I just got in, and I had to see you immediately. There is no time to lose. Then again, with these demon matters, that always seems to be the case. I'm caught up in something I don't really know what to do with. There are so many questions."

The priest had no idea what Wally was talking about, but he knew it had to be something big for the man to fly out from the Vatican in the middle of the night. He studied him curiously and noted that he clutched his leather bag to his dripping clothes. Damian sighed and went to fetch a second towel.

He handed it to Wally, took his bag, and set it beside him on the floor. "Dry yourself off and calm down. I'll make us some tea, okay?"

His friend looked at the towel in bemusement and nodded. Damian smiled and hurried to the kitchen. He ignited the gas stove, filled the kettle, and set it on to boil. While he set two cups out, he glanced wearily through the doorway. Wally now sat by the fire with his bag in his lap. He clutched it tightly to his chest, staring at the flames.

The man twitched and muttered to himself. Damian knew the researcher was the nervous type, but he had never seen him quite so bad before. The tea kettle whistled for attention. The priest poured the hot water into the teapot and closed the lid, letting it steep as he loaded a tray and carried it into the living room. He set the tray on the table, pulled the bottle of vodka from the small bar, and filled a shot glass. Tea would warm his visitor, but the liquor would calm him…hopefully.

Damian held the shot out to Wally. His friend blinked but took it from him, not arguing as the priest had expected. He swallowed and grimaced before handing the glass back. His gaze returned to the fire as his host poured the tea and watched him closely.

Even Ravi could tell something was awry. *This guy either witnessed a massacre or performed one.*

Damian ignored her, carefully handed Wally a cup, and sat down opposite him with his own tea. Wally took a sip and released a deep breath, the warmth easing the damp chill. The priest gave him a few moments to settle. Forcing him to talk before he was ready would only make things worse. He needed to calm his nerves to a coherent level.

After a few minutes, Wally shifted his gaze to Damian as he shook his head and sighed again. "I'm sorry. I'm a mess."

Damian laughed and stood to refill both cups before he sat and crossed his legs. "We're all messes these days. What's going on?"

Wally put his cup and saucer on the side table and stared at his bag. "So, I went to the post office this morning to check my box for any family mail. I set it up so work wouldn't be inundated during the holidays, since I have a big family. On top of that, anything that comes through the Vatican is read before its given to me."

Damian frowned. "That's good to know. It's like being in prison."

The researcher shrugged. "I suppose it's not a terrible thing. A lot of hate mail is sent there. Anyway, I sat down to go through my post and found a flat package at the bottom. It was wrapped in a single piece of brown paper, and the tape that sealed it had bloody fingerprints. There was no return address and no note inside, so I have no idea who sent it. The stamp didn't reflect an exact mailing location. I swear it was almost like it was put there by hand."

"Curious. Does that happen to you often?"

Wally shook his head. "Not in my personal post. People send relics anonymously all the time, but this was my private box. Obviously, I opened it immediately. Inside, I found several of the cardinal's effects—the one who'd had the relic in his room. Among those was an extensive set of thin leather-bound journals, all handwritten by the cardinal. They even had his seal on them, which I found odd for a private journal. Nonetheless, there they were."

The visitor put his leather bag on the floor, opened the front pouch, and shoved a change of clothes aside. He pulled the package out and unwrapped the brown paper carefully. Damian leaned forward, staring at the journals on top. Wally was right. The cardinal's personal crest was burned into the front cover of every single one of them. They were held closed by a thin piece of leather tied in a knot.

Wally pushed them aside to reveal several other items and the bloody fingerprints on the wrapping. Damian leaned back and rubbed his hand across his chin, intensely curious. His friend handed the package over, and the priest placed it on the footstool in front of him and stared at it.

The researcher cleared his throat and crossed his legs, water still dripping from his pants. "I didn't take those things to the church since I couldn't explain why I had them. On top of that, I could tell someone had gone to great lengths to get them to me privately. I didn't feel I should turn them over to the church unless I understood why."

Damian gave him a comforting smile and patted his leg. "You did the right thing, Wally. I know it might not feel that way, but you are ultimately protecting them right now —at least, until you understand what's going on here."

Wally's shoulders relaxed at Damian's reassurance.

"After I got home, I put everything in freezer bags to keep them dry and safe, and caught a plane. Luckily it was my day off, so I didn't need to explain the trip to anyone. That's why I'm so late. I grabbed the first available flight."

Damian leaned back again and stared into the fire. "You did the right thing," he said again. "Do you have any idea what this might mean? Why would they want *you*, the keeper of secrets, to have this rather than the church?"

The researcher shook his head. "I really have no idea. I wanted to read everything to see if it gave me any clues, but I know that I can't keep them with me at the Vatican. The risk of them being found is too high. I wouldn't be able to explain."

The priest nodded and suppressed any outward expression of concern. He stood and put his hand out. "Come. You should stay the night. You won't find a flight back this late, and it's not safe to wander around London in this storm. I have a spare room upstairs with a hot shower and dry clothes."

Wally paused for a moment before he grasped Damian's hand. "I suppose you're right. I'm off tomorrow too, so I can take my time and not be frozen and wet."

Damian put his arm around his friend's shoulder and led him up the stairs and to the room. He paused at the bedroom door as Wally put his things down and began peeling his layers off. "If you need anything—anything at all—let me know. I'll probably be up for a while, so call for me or come down. You did the correct thing, Wally."

The nervous man gave him a tight-lipped smile. "I really hope you're right."

CHAPTER TWO

Damian hesitated at the foot of the stairs, and his gaze drifted to the living room. Shadows from the fireplace danced across the ceiling, and the pounding of the rain echoed. Thankfully the thunder and lightning had stopped, which would calm Wally a little. The poor man was spooked enough from receiving the package in the mail without the added stress of the storm. Whoever sent it had an agenda, but the researcher wasn't one to dig into mysteries outside of his job. The reasonable explanation was perhaps that whoever sent it knew he would bring it to Damian.

Ravi sniffed. *This is an interesting turn of events.*

The priest crept toward his chair, drawn by the open package on the footstool. *Yeah, it is, but possibly not surprising. Let's take a look.*

Fine, but be careful, she said. *I don't have a good feeling about it.*

Damian sat and shuffled the bags, taking a quick look at each. Starting with the smallest, he emptied the contents into his hand. A round medallion the size of the bottom of a teacup slid out, old and slightly rusted. He used his hand-kerchief to rub the metal, then held it close to his face. *Interesting symbol. I've never seen it before. You?*

The demon strained to look through his eyes. *No. It looks like something you'd pick up at a casino, only morbid.*

He dropped the disc back into the bag. *I doubt our cardinal is a showgirl's kind of man.*

Ravi scoffed. *You say that, but he's also suspected of demonology. For all you know, bro could be shacked up in a penthouse suite with seven ladies of the night.*

Damian shook his head and looked at the other items. He pulled a book from a plastic sleeve and flipped through it—a book on demons with notes scribbled in the corners. He read one of them out loud. "*Asamta gibia rhum…*"

Ravi gasped when he'd finished. *That's Aramaic. It trans-lates to something like "laying of the hands for chosen people." Weird.*

He raised an eyebrow when he realized how much translation would be required. He replaced the book and moved on. *We'll take a closer look at that later.*

The demon snickered. *I told you he was laying on the hands…in Vegas.*

Damian chuckled and set aside several robes, each with different symbols stitched into them. Beneath those were a map and the five journals bound together. He ran his finger over the symbols burned beneath the cardinal's crest on the front. *I have never seen these before, but they share qual-ities with some we have uncovered. Do they look familiar to you?*

Ravi thought for a silent moment. *The top one has ties to a cult, one from centuries ago that was apparently deeply connected with Lucifer. They were said to be the first to bring demons to Earth. The others...no, they don't look familiar to me at all.*

The priest was slightly disappointed. Every time he turned, he encountered something that no one had ever seen before. *I swear these symbols are like university fraternities. There are about a thousand, with new ones popping up everywhere. I should gather all the different symbols and put them in one text for the generations to come.*

The demon yawned. *It's not like you have to register these bitches. The cults don't pay taxes, that's for sure.*

Bastards. Maybe we would go a bit lighter on them if they gave back to the community instead of snatching souls. Give some fucking money to the highway system, assholes. You have to drive your beater over them to get to your next sacrifice.

Ravi giggled. *This highway is sponsored by the Ancient Followers of Lucifer. Keep our roadways clean.*

Damian grinned, picked up the last journal, and saw the date on the first page—October 14, 1965. *Huh. These date back a ways.*

She sniffed. *I mean, the cardinal is older than hell. He probably had tea with Jesus at some point.*

The priest leaned back, held the journal open, and stared down at the very precise cursive handwriting on the first page. He began to read, trying to put himself in the cardinal's place. It was written in Latin, but he translated.

October 14, 1965

This is a new journal, the others now full to the brim. It is October yet again, the witching month. My skin crawls every time the clock strikes midnight. I wait here for him, wondering if he will reappear. Will he find me lacking in my duties, in my restitution for the sin I have taken upon my shoulders? Yet, night after night, the clock ticks past the hour and no one comes.

The thunder of the storm outside rattles this small parish in the Italian countryside. I am here on assignment, an investigation into the recent surge in demon activity. Every time the bishop looks at me, I wonder if he knows. I keep it hidden. The secrets are mine to the grave or until they find me out.

At night, I lay there somewhere between waking and dreaming. My dreams are no longer my own but are filled with visions of the events of the past. I see the blood run along the streets and the fire, and I hear the screams. I hear her and I run to her, but she is no longer there. I clutch my crucifix, only to find a medallion in its place, one that holds his crest. Never have I seen this in waking hours, but it is clear in my mind.

When I wake, sweat covers my forehead, and I can feel the pain from my old wound surge through my body. It burns like the talons that stabbed me. It was all in the name of God, I know, but sometimes it feels as if I am no longer under His protection. Was that a side effect of the deal I made? Will I be forsaken until death? What then? Have I given away my seat with the angels to save a precious entity of God? It will be worth it, even for an eternity of suffering. It is my job, after all. I serve God's Will and the church.

Let's hope the silent nights remain that way. I do not hurry to fulfill my end of the bargain. Until I write again.

Ye Yalufa,

Mortimore

Damian read the last line again, repeating it in a whisper. "'Ye Yalufa.' I don't know that phrase."

Ravi sniffed and came forward. *Oh, that's Aramaic as well. It means "Your Disciple." He either dreams he is much more important to God than he is, or there is more to this story.*

The priest closed the book and stared into the fire. *I have a sneaking suspicion we'll find out a lot more from these journals. I doubt it is as simple as a case of mistaken divinity. He speaks like a fearful man.*

And one who seems remorseful, yet proud of his past. Something happened, but I can't grasp what he is talking about.

Damian tapped his fingers. *Me either.*

The demon yawned loudly. *Maybe it's time for a little whiskey to calm the senses.*

He shook his head, slightly distracted by the strange events. *I think I'll stick to tea tonight. I can still feel the pounding on the door in the back of my skull.*

As he ran his thumb over the symbol thunder rumbled loudly, making him jump. His heart pulsed rapidly, and he rubbed his arms and shook his head. *I feel like this night has unhinged me. Every time I move, something pops up or jumps out at me.*

Ravi agreed. *I don't usually get spooked, but I have to admit this day has me by the short hairs.*

Damian laughed. *Imagine that, a demon afraid of the creepy. Isn't that what you guys are made of?*

She snickered. *Oh yeah—a little death, a little malice, and a pinch of creepy. You figured the recipe out.*

We are letting our imaginations get the best of us. Maybe it's time to call it a night? Start fresh when there is more sunlight and less storm.

He stood and stretched, pushed the doors to the fireplace closed, and began to pack the items into the brown paper. As he gathered the journals, he paused and rubbed at the crest once again. *I can't help but wonder if the cardinal is still alive at this point. All this seems very dangerous, and none of it excuses his crimes.*

Ravi clicked her tongue. *Be careful about the conclusions you draw. Demons are tricky. They can turn your head in a heartbeat. We don't have any clue who sent this. It could have been some random neighbor, or it could have been Lucifer.*

Do they have mail in hell? No wonder packages take so long!

No, but if we did, I'm sure we would figure out some way to send demons in a box.

Damian picked up the stack of items and walked toward the bookcase. *Oh, look, little Cindy, someone sent you a present for your birthday!*

The demon laughed and finished his thought. *Is it a Barbie? Is it a pony? Nope. It's Moloch, here to take your soul and eat your bones. Special party tricks for an extra cost.*

The priest shivered and pressed his hand against the back wall of the shelf. It clicked, and the whole thing swung open to reveal a hidden safe. He entered the code and set the items inside, staring at them for a moment before closing it again. Ravi was surprised that he was putting them under lock and key. *You getting paranoid?*

Damian locked the safe and returned the shelf to its position. *A stranger sent highly valuable information to our friend, who brought it to us. We don't know if this is a trick. I'm the only one who knows about this safe, and for now, I think it's smart to keep it that way. I want time to research these items and delve into those journals before someone comes looking for them.*

Ravi went quiet for a moment. *You mean the Catholic church, don't you?*

He hated the idea, but it wasn't ridiculous. The church was known for protecting their secrets and doing anything they had to, to accomplish that. If they knew he had those pieces of the cardinal's life, his home would be turned upside down in a search. It was better that they were out of sight and that Max didn't get wind of them, at least not yet. There were things in the world that he wasn't ready to reveal to his mentee—things he'd learned long ago that had shattered his view of the world they lived in.

Damian swigged the last of his tea, then carried the dishes to the kitchen and took the time to wash everything and put it all away. While he worked, his mind considered the words of the journal entry. He knew he could sit all night reading, but this was not the night to do so. His body was tired and ready for sleep, and he wanted to talk to the researcher in the morning. He had a million questions, but he knew he needed to limit their scope. Wally was his friend, and the man had risked great danger to bring him those things. Any more information would make the nervous keeper of secrets a liability to others and put Damian himself at risk.

Ravi yawned again. *Do you think this cardinal is into something bad?*

The priest narrowed his eyes as he clicked the living room lights off. *It doesn't sound like anything good, that's for sure, although I sense he is not the villain in this story, at least not deliberately.*

The demon agreed but said nothing more, leading Damian to believe she was holding something back. Then again, she seemed a pro at doing that, and he knew pushing her would only make her retreat even more. He moved upstairs and crept quietly down the hall. Opening the spare bedroom door slightly, he peeked in on Wally, who lay sound asleep in his bed. The man had been exhausted, and a safe, warm bed had been exactly what he needed.

Damian closed the door and headed down to his room. He changed for bed and shivered as he climbed between the cold sheets. The thunder rumbled again overhead as questions flooded his mind. Who was the woman the cardinal had written of? What had he done that was so bad that he waited each night for a terrifying visitor to arrive on his doorstep?

Ravi groaned. *Can we talk about something other than Creepy McCardinal? I will be up all night if we don't.*

The priest raised his eyebrows and smiled. *Yes, we can. In fact, I think I might need that too. What did you have in mind?*

The demon spoke immediately. *Well, I remembered that shopping trip you said you would take me on.*

Damian grumbled and turned over. *Maybe I was wrong. Maybe the cardinal's story isn't as frightening as I thought.*

Ravi giggled. *Nope, you can't get out of this. We need to set a date. You promised, and you know that the longer you hold out, the worse it will be for you.*

He rolled his eyes. *Fine. We can go tomorrow afternoon. But I saw some of the London fashions on the television. You cannot dress me in anything that belongs in a demon chamber, and if there is a skirt involved, I'm out. I don't need a breeze when fighting demons.*

She laughed loudly. *Don't worry. I scratched skirts off the list a while ago. I don't really want to see that. You have knobby knees, so we'll stick with velour.*

The priest pulled the pillow over his head. *Lord, help me.*
It's too late for that, honey.

CHAPTER THREE

Damian glanced at his watch as he finished pouring the freshly dripped coffee. It was already eleven, and Wally had, shockingly, woken only an hour before. He turned to his visitor and held one of the cups out. The researcher looked a lot better than he had the night before. His eyes were bright again, the bags were almost gone, and the color had returned to his cheeks. Damian could tell he was glad to have the cardinal's items out of his care.

The priest nodded toward the door. "Shall we enjoy the sunlight? For once, it isn't raining."

Wally nodded, taking a sip. "After you."

They sat at the table in the empty courtyard. It was an unusually warm fall day, and Damian enjoyed it more than ever. He felt he needed the light to pull the dank, dark mood of the night before from his soul. He closed his eyes as he took a long slurp.

Wally glanced at the blue sky for a moment before speaking. "So, did you read any of the journals last night?"

Damian smirked. "You know I couldn't *not*. I only read one page, though. It seems there are more out there, but October 1965 is the earliest we have, from what I saw when I flipped through. I'm not sure if the others fall in a timeline after that, but I'll get there."

The researcher nodded, his eyes afraid. "And what did you find out from the page you read?"

The priest sighed and shrugged. "It was very cryptic and contained little detail. He did something for a woman, and it seems he made a deal with a nefarious creature to do so. While he questioned his eternity, he reaffirmed his devotion at the same time. He sounded like a fearful man after some severe event. Like I said, though, there weren't many details, so it's a complete mystery what he was talking about."

Wally sipped his coffee, seemingly unaffected. "I thought there would be something bigger than what I've heard. Hopefully, you can find that information. I knew you'd be the one to figure it out."

Damian smiled and drew a deep breath. "So, why don't you call your superiors and take a few days off? Stay around London, relax, and see the sights?"

Wally groaned. "I wish I could. It sounds wonderful. Unfortunately, things at the church have been very hush-hush and eerie recently, and the last thing I need to do is suddenly disappear. I don't want to draw any attention to myself. Besides, I'm the only one running the artifacts room down below, so they need me there. We have a constant stream of pieces coming in."

The clang of the gate caught their attention. Max grunted and fumbled an armful of books. Damian chuckled and hurried to rescue the top of the stack. "I didn't realize you were awake, much less out and about already."

The young man eased his books onto the table and wiped his forehead, panting. "I couldn't sleep this morning. Partly because of my mind, and the other part because of my rotten demon."

Astaroth scoffed. *Oh, you mean the one who keeps your puny ass alive? My apologies, master.*

Max ignored the smart-ass comment and tapped the books. "I had a blast touring a couple of weeks ago, so I went to the library to research historical locations I could visit. There are a million places I haven't seen in this world, and if I have time here and there, I could jet off and explore."

Damian smirked. "It looks like I created a monster. Next thing I know, you'll buy an old VW van and hit the road with only your pack and your demon."

The young priest grinned without shame. "Yeah, I guess I'm hooked now, but curiosity is a good thing. The way the demons destroy stuff, none of us know how long these places will remain. Better see them while I can."

Astaroth sniffed. *Wait, is that my deep Columbian blend they are frivolously sipping? I swear to God, I am running a coffee shop for the entire damn church.*

Max glanced at the cups. *Will you relax? It's coffee. We can't possibly drink it all. Besides, you already found four other shops you want to buy from.*

The demon scoffed. *Damn right I did. I won't waste this trip to Earth, not when the idiots below are destroying everything. I have to find some sort of metal lockbox to keep my coffee in. Grubby fingers will rue the day they messed with my beans.*

Max did his best not to roll his eyes. He smiled uncomfortably at Wally, unsure who he was. Damian noticed and shook his head. "Oh, how rude of me. Max, this is Father Wally Okenhoff, a good friend of mine from the Vatican. Wally, this is my trainee and partner Max."

The young man shook his hand with a quick look of realization. "Oh, Father Wally. Yes, you're the one we traveled to Rome for Damian to visit. I wasn't aware you were coming to see us."

The researcher shuffled nervously in his seat, his gaze darting to Damian's. "I thought no one knew about that trip."

Damian patted his friend on the shoulder. "Relax, old friend. Max is completely trustworthy. He doesn't know what the visit pertained to, and I trust him with my life."

Max looked appreciative at the comment and nodded. "Secrets are buried with me, sir."

Wally eyed him for a moment, then relaxed. "Of course. Anyone Damian trusts, I do as well. Nice to meet you."

"Are you staying for a while?"

The researcher looked at his watch and gulped the last of his coffee. "Actually, no. Unfortunately, I need to be on my way to catch a flight. I haven't even purchased my ticket yet, and I know today is a busy traveling day."

He stood, clutching his bag in front of him. Damian lifted an eyebrow at the worn satchel. He sure was protective of the thing. *I wonder what else is in that bag? He protects it like he has the Virgin Mary in there.*

Ravi chuckled. *Probably the souls of thirteen virgins or*

something creepy like that. Maybe it's Beelzebub's right pinky toe that was cut off in the war.

The priest pressed his lips tightly together to hold back a laugh. "Shall I walk you to the gate? I can call you a cab."

Wally nodded and waved at Max. "No need to call a cab. I'm sure if I walk a few blocks, I'll find one."

Damian opened the gate and stepped into the street with him. They stood there for a moment, looking around. The priest cleared his throat. "Thank you for entrusting me with what you have. You can be sure that I will protect the journals and the secrets they hold with my life."

Wally smiled and tugged his hat down. "I know you will. I wouldn't have come here if I thought otherwise. Whatever is in there may give you a clue as to where to find the cardinal. I think at this point, it might help us all if we knew. Then again, I have been wrong before."

Damian waved as a cab drove toward them. It pulled up to the curb, and he opened the door for his visitor. Wally tossed his bag into the back seat, and the men shook hands firmly. The researcher leaned in and whispered, "Be careful. Some secrets are worth more than others. Blood has been spilled over the centuries in an attempt to hide the truth. This would not be the first or the last time."

The priest nodded as his friend tipped his hat and climbed inside. Damian shut the door with a twinge of fear from that ominous warning. The cab pulled away and disappeared down the street. Damian stood on the curb and looked at the gathering clouds. One thing he knew for sure was that secrets in the church were more dangerous than most.

Max shook his head, excited about all the places he wanted to visit. "Man, I did not realize how many cool spots are out there. In Vietnam, there is a place called the Golden Bridge. It is literally two stone hands holding up a golden walking bridge like something from a fairy tale. Then there's Petra. That place is crazy! It's a historical archaeological city in southern Jordan. They filmed *Indiana Jones* there, the one about the Holy Grail."

Damian nodded. "Yes, *The Last Crusade*. 'Only a penitent man can pass.'"

The trainee laughed. "Yes! Then the guy drinks out of the wrong grail and his skin melts off. Loved that when I was a kid."

"It was a good scene, although I wasn't a kid when it came out." Damian sipped his coffee and laughed. "Okay, where else?"

Max rubbed his chin for a moment. "The Acropolis—the city with the temple to Athena. And of course, La Sagrada Familia. The temple of all temples built by the Catalan genius, Antoni Gaudi. Such a wonder to behold, don't you think?"

"You *have* done your research," Damian said. "Tell me what has captured your attention so strongly about each of these places, young Max."

The young priest eyed him for a moment, wondering if he was ribbing him. Even if he was, Max didn't care. He was excited about his discoveries. "There is so much history in these places. They date back to times we can never grasp. I mean, history tells us some of the story, but we can only imagine how the world actually was back then."

"That's for sure," Damian agreed.

Max nodded. "The Golden Bridge was built because the artist wanted people to feel the connection between God and the Earth. The hands are literally sculpted to be God's. Petra is a historical wonder because it's intact in so many ways while others from that time period are not. The Acropolis revealed a city among cities, a basis for our current day societies. And La Sagrada is a beautiful oath to a faithful family built in brick and stone, reaching toward the heavens."

Damian smiled, liking the enthusiasm Max had for the world. It was something easily lost, especially in their line of work. They saw so much of the ugly side of things, and it was important to see the beauty, too.

The young priest continued, spurred by his own excitement. "There are so many secret nuances to these places, and I want to touch and feel them. Maybe, even if only for a moment, to feel as if I were there during that time of innovation, art, and thought. I feel like we don't do those things anymore. I sometimes feel like this planet has lost that luster."

His mentor leaned forward and rested his chin on his clasped hands. "I love your enthusiasm, but it's important you understand that some things aren't what they seem. It helps you to take disappointment in stride and find wonder in the rest."

Max leaned back, narrowing his eyes. "Like what?"

"Well, let's start with the Golden Bridge. Those hands were not carved. They were actually the hands of a

Leviathan named Artrus employed by Lucifer and sent centuries before to rid the world of humans. During a battle between him and the Archangel Gabriel, the Leviathan was turned to stone. His body disintegrated, but his hands fell into the grass and were left as a reminder. The Vietnamese built a bridge through them and attempted to hide the truth from the people with a made-up story. Over time, Artrus became an old wives' tale and nothing more."

Max scoffed. "Man, those are an alien's hands? Talk about getting it wrong."

Damian eased his neck to release the tension. "Well, yes and no. If you think about it, they *are* a representation of God's hands and the smack-down he delivers when you attack his people."

The trainee chortled. "I suppose you're right. Okay, what else?"

"Petra. The Nabataeans were thought to be magical and lived in the desert with few problems. The other tribes didn't know that they were actually demons disguised as humans, there to fight the Arabs. Ultimately, they lost, but not without many human casualties. As far as the Acropolis is concerned, I have no knowledge beyond what history tells us."

Max sighed. "Thank God. Please tell me you don't have a story about the Sagrada Familia."

Damian smirked evilly, and the young priest threw his hands in the air.

"I like this story the most," Damian said. "It shows the progression of demon hunting. In the La Sagrada Familia, there are seven towers. The tower of the Virgin Mary was later renovated because it was originally used as a dungeon to house Damned until they were killed by various means. When the church realized that some people could be exorcised, they were ashamed. They immediately changed the tower to the Virgin Mary—the misunderstood."

"Wow, that's crazy. I didn't see that one coming. So, the Familia is actually a story about our faults. About our changes within the war with the demons."

Damian nodded. "That is correct. Even we humans can learn new tricks once in a while."

Astaroth snarked, *I wish you could learn to shut up.*

CHAPTER FOUR

Damian stared at himself in the mirror. In one of the small dressing rooms in the back of a high-fashion haberdashery in London, he swallowed hard and turned, trying to give the outfit a chance. The thigh-length jacket was thick like a peacoat and adorned with close-ups of bright red roses. His eyes slid to the matching pants, which had a slightly smaller print.

Ravi oohed. *That's all the rage right now. You look good in prints.*

The priest gaped at himself, closed his mouth, then gaped again. *Ravi, I look like Elton John on a bad day. In fact, I'm sure if I wore this out of here, I'd be attacked by bees and birds trying to collect my nectar.*

She choked on her laughter. *Right. Okay. Let's move on, then.*

Damian carefully removed the coat and gave it a final glare, knowing full well it probably cost more than his first car. The next outfit seemed more subdued on the hanger, but he chuckled once he'd put it on. The top was a single piece separated in front to look like a jacket and matching shirt. Pictures rolled over the shoulders, down the sleeves, and across the midsection. Damian narrowed his eyes and studied the image, which resembled a gray and white rendition of the rings of Saturn.

Ravi was silent, waiting for his reaction. The pants sported the same rings of disaster and ended three inches above his ankles. *I know it rains a lot in London, but seriously, is this necessary?*

The demon huffed lightly. *If you don't like your ankles showing, wear your boots with it—or buy some new ones, preferably.*

Damian hurried to undress. *Next! I prefer to keep my ankles covered and not make others nauseous with my rings of death.*

Rings of— Ugh, you're hopeless.

He rehung the outfit and reached for another. *I prefer to think of myself as practical, not hopeless.*

The priest studied the next choice with one brow raised. *I think we grabbed this one by mistake. It obviously came from the old woman section of Petites Plus. This jacket is pink velour with birds and some sort of purple bush on it. And I won't even comment on these pants. Seriously, it looks like a page from* Where's Waldo.

Ravi groaned. *Fine! But you're trying the next one. No comments until it's on.*

Damian moved the velour aside, slipped the next top over his head, and zipped the front. There weren't any armholes. Biting back a sarcastic comment, he grabbed what felt like a bearskin rug from the hanger, wrapped it around himself, and looked in the mirror. The top resembled a tent designed as a 1970s waterproof track jacket without arms. The bottoms? He grimaced. A striped fur skirt overlapped in the front and hung to his shins.

Ravi giggled. *That was one of the biggest hits by Estelita Mendonça last winter.*

He stared at his reflection in disbelief. *I also believe it was one of the biggest hits for the man lost in the woods two years ago.*

The demon ignored him. *You can kick ass, stay dry, be fashionable, and keep warm all at the same time. What did you call it? Practical.*

Damian shook his head. *Okay, enough of this shit show for one day. I gave you a chance, but this is utterly ridiculous.*

She groaned. *Okay. Okay. One more. I promise you will like it. And that's not wishful thinking. If you hate it, we leave, and you'll never hear another word from me.*

Damian clipped the rug skirt to the hanger and folded his arms. *Fine. One more. But only if it doesn't have any inflatable parts, anything resembling animal hair, a sheen, and isn't woven with locks of a newborn's hair.*

Agreed. It's in the suit bag on the left.

He grunted, and the dressing room curtain billowed as he changed one last time. Damian buttoned the pants and rolled his shoulders back. *You'd think they'd give you more than three square feet to change in.*

Ravi laughed. *Take a look.*

The priest rolled his eyes and faced the mirror, instantly losing his annoyed face. He tilted his head and pulled down on the tailored jacket. The suit was pale gray with a slight sheen, but it had a James Bond flair. The white button-up tucked into the front, and the pants were perfectly pressed. *Well, hot damn, look at this! Classic, well-fitting, and suave.*

The demon chirped excitedly, *I told you. It's Armani.*

He nodded his head, impressed. *I could even wear my suspenders and bowtie with it.*

Ravi agreed. *Yep, and it would bring those two items into this century. I would suggest a better trench, but baby steps, I suppose.*

Damian lifted an eyebrow. *Yes, baby steps. I like my trench coats, and they all have the special hidden storage I need. They should make a line of clothes for our profession.*

I'm afraid the turnover of people in your profession might be too high for a profit.

True. Well, Ravi, I have to admit, I love this suit. It's the best thing I've tried on in years.

She clicked her tongue. *I have a feeling it's one of the very few things you've tried on in years.*

Damian ignored her comment. *I will be honest. I didn't think there was a chance in hell I would find anything I liked today. I seriously came only because I keep my promises and had made one to you to go shopping. I thought it would be an exhausting bust. Well done, at least on this one. I wish you had started with it, though.*

Ravi laughed. *Well, I'll take this as a win. At least it's a start, and now I know your style—classic and chic. Not really what I imagined a man of God wearing, but hey, everyone likes to look good.*

He stripped and dressed in the clothes he'd arrived in. *Very true. I bet even Gabriel would fancy a suit like this.*

She scoffed but didn't reply. Damian hung the suit neatly on the hanger and zipped the bag, then slung it over his arm and made sure he had everything. *Do I leave these here?*

Yep. Take what you're buying up to the front. I have to say, I liked that coat you tried on first.

Damian shivered. *Are you serious? That coat had a tail. A tail! Men of God don't wear tails, and I don't mean the fancy tuxedo kind. There was fur involved.*

Ravi chuckled as he pulled the curtain back. On the hanger was a bright-white winter fur coat. Wisps of purples, pinks, and blues along the seams were tied at the back into a long unicorn tail. The sparkles were enough to make him retch. He couldn't even imagine what Katie would say if she knew he'd vaguely considered the thing, if only to please his demon.

Damian stopped abruptly at a rack of bowties. *They are selling these again? You told me they were out of style.*

Ravi was serious. *No. I told you* yours *were out of style. In fact, bowties seem to be all the rage now, but you have to know when to let go of plaid. And the one with the ducks on it is seriously creepy.*

The priest frowned. *I like the ducks. But my favorite is the one with the crosses. That was a huge hit at my sermons in Vegas.*

Ravi was silent for a moment. *Oh, so you busted it out at the church sermons? That sounds riveting, really. I'm shocked you don't have a following. Whatever did they do without you there?*

He shrugged. *I guess the place was a little less fashionable after I left.*

She giggled as he approached the counter to pay for the suit. The cashier was super-nice, especially when he paid the three-thousand-dollar price in cash. She made sure his suit hung perfectly and zipped the bag up, thanking him for the hundredth time. Damian left the store feeling overwhelmed by the snobbery. He breathed deeply, and cold air filled his lungs.

His gaze settled on a small eatery down the block. *Let's get a bite and coffee, shall we?*

I'm hungry. Why not?

Damian ordered a sandwich and an iced coffee and sat at one of the small café tables outside. He loved that time of year, and the cool breeze refreshed him more than the coffee did. With his legs crossed comfortably, he people-watched and enjoyed his lunch while Ravi commented randomly on some of the clothes. Everyone was dressed in the same styles he had laughed at in the store.

He sipped his coffee as a man walked by in the fur skirt. *I feel like I have traveled through time to a city with a bunch of weird space-people. Do they actually wear this shit to fucking jobs? Like, what do they do for a living? Do they perform surgery in the seven-layer shredded blouse they purchased for fifteen hundred dollars?*

Ravi yawned. *Will you kick ass in your three-grand suit?*

Damian nodded and swallowed the last of his sandwich. *I will, but I won't look stupid doing it. And I won't accidentally put my eye out with my shoulder pad.*

The demon laughed delightedly, and Damian smiled as he sipped his coffee. *I want to ask you something off-topic.*

What? she asked. *And no, there is not a special breed of animal they kill for that skirt. It's faux fur. Real fur is totally out.*

Damian smirked. *No, I wanted to ask if you could tell me anything about the book with Pandora's—or Lilith's—signature in it.*

She was silent for a moment. *I really don't know if I should discuss Lilith. Her life is her business. I don't need to be caught up in something like that.*

The priest could sense she was afraid of Katie's demon. *Remember, Pandora is my friend. She would never do anything to you. Besides, I promise I won't say a thing to her about whatever you tell me. I don't really want to tell her I've got this book, anyway. I wouldn't even know what questions to ask her. She tends to be stubborn about answering questions about her past— not that I know anyone else like that.*

Ravi ignored his jibe. She opened up when she determined it was safe and reasonable. *All right. Well, do you know the biblical story of Lilith?*

The Jewish version? Not too well, no.

She cleared her throat. *They believe that she was the first woman on Earth, and was created as a companion for Adam. At first it all seemed well and good, but as time went by, she resented Adam's control and wanted to be more expressive sexually, emotionally, and in every way, really. She lashed out at him and ran when she saw that she had gone too far. It is said that God sent the angels to track her down, but she had already changed and became one of the first demons on Earth. From there, stories circulated that she took the souls of children and ate babies, but nothing was ever proven.*

Damian smirked. *It seems like a possibility to me.*

Ravi chuckled and continued. *There was no word of Lilith*

for a long time after that, then we heard whispers that she was wandering, finding her place in and out of humans. Sometimes, she would wander for decades and then fall back into hell and spend time there. About five hundred or so years ago, it emerged that she had been taken as a bride by Lucifer. At first, no one thought much of it, but Lucifer was obsessed and dubbed her the Queen of hell. She was the almighty standing at the side of the almighty, at least down below. She ruled with force; it was almost as if something happened to push all her anger out.

Damian listened, finding the account curious. It seemed to fit Pandora, but there was way more depth to her story than he had ever imagined. Ravi spoke with certainty, especially about the later years. *She ruled with Lucifer for a long time, but rumor has it one day she was gone. She left him and returned to Earth. I heard her brother tricked her, trying to make her human so he could kill her. He was always jealous of her.*

He laughed. *He wanted to be Lucifer's bride?*

Ravi giggled. *Can you imagine?*

Well, his plan backfired on him.

So it did. I was shocked when T'Chezz's head was severed from his neck. It was a big deal for many demons, and probably angels, too. There were many times through history when we heard nothing about Lilith, and no one really knows where she was during those times. Some say with God, others say roaming the Earth. Wherever it was, she stayed low-key.

Damian scoffed. *Low-key sounds like an oxymoron for someone like Pandora. Did you ever meet her?*

Ravi fell silent, and Damian waited. After a few moments, she spoke quietly. *Yes, but it was only for a brief moment and far too long ago for me to really remember. My accounts are mostly from what we hear in hell. I had an admin job, so I got the skinny. Anyway, so yeah, that's the whole story.*

He was surprised at how quickly she stopped the conversation but could tell she wouldn't divulge more. The questions racked up in his head, and he wondered if they would ever be answered.

CHAPTER FIVE

*T*his one has a stronger burnt taste, indicating a higher *caffeine content. I discern hints of char, a bit of chocolate, and a smoky finish. I would say this is the K7, grown in Africa. It's a selection of French Mission Bourbon selected at Legelet Estate in Muhoroni, Kenya. I like it, though not on a daily basis.* Astaroth was explaining the taste of the coffee Max had just sipped.

The two had signed up for a tasting a few blocks from the house, where coffees from all over the world were available. Astaroth was good at it, and Max could basically tell it was coffee. The priest moved to the next cup and sipped. *How about that one?*

The demon hummed to himself. *This is a tricky one. It's definitely an arabica. Hmm. It has a rich, full-bodied flavor. It's well balanced in acidity, and there are multidimensional hints here. I would say...Sulawesi Toraja Kalossi from Sulawesi, Indonesia.*

Max flipped the card. *You're absolutely right. Dang, how do you do that?*

It's all about relaxing the taste buds and going with it. Okay, you try. Put on the blindfold and start in the middle.

Max lifted the blindfold and hesitated. *Are you sure? I'm terrible at this.*

Astaroth chuckled. *I'm sure you will be green, but nothing too bad.*

The priest shrugged pulled the mask on. He ran his fingers over the cup in front of him, picked it up, and sniffed the brew. Carefully, he took a sip, running his tongue through the hot liquid. Astaroth waited for him to swallow. *All right, rookie, what do you think?*

Max cleared his throat and tried to concentrate. *Well, I taste some deep...char. And a hint of...basil? Oh, and I can taste the acid bubbling in it. I say it's a fire brew from Hawaii.*

Astaroth sighed. *Are you completely braindead? You just described some sort of pasta sauce. That is the Interspecific hybrid, Timor from India. How could you screw up that badly? And what is with the basil?*

He removed the blindfold and shrugged. *I told you I was terrible at this. And we've been here for five hours. I seriously feel like my heart might burst out of my chest and fall to the floor. It wouldn't even stop beating. It would grab a cup of coffee and run off.*

The demon groaned. *Fine, let's go. I don't need you to have a complete caffeine stroke-out here in the store. You would embarrass the hell out of me.*

Max smiled at the guy behind the counter as he collected his coat and hat, nodded at the staff, and left. He stuck one hand in his pocket and gripped the large bag of coffee they had purchased tightly with the other to ease the feeling that his whole body was shaking. As he walked, he swayed to the side, looking like a drunk leaving a bar. He steadied himself on a bench for a moment, trying to calm the heart that now felt like it was in his throat.

Astaroth scoffed. *Lightweight. You can't even handle a five-hour coffee- tasting. I have always said, if you can't handle your caffeine, you shouldn't drink and drive. That is how high-speed accidents happen.*

Max put his hand out to hail a cab. *No need to worry about that, but you might want to focus on keeping me from puking in the back of this cab. Good Lord, I feel like I had one too many shots with Damian.*

The demon laughed loudly. *Wait until the hangover hits you. When the crash comes, you'll drop wherever you stand. You might as well know, you could become an addict.*

He rolled his eyes as the cabbie pulled out toward the row house. *Great. I'll walk around chewing coffee beans, looking for my next brew.*

That's the good stuff.

Damian smiled kindly at the woman behind the counter of the store he had just entered. After lunch, he decided to indulge Ravi a little more since she had been so helpful with the information on Pandora. He knew she hadn't told the whole truth, but that would hopefully come in time. If shopping didn't help her open up, nothing would at that point.

He walked down the aisle of shoes until he found the

men's section, which displayed dress shoes of all types and designs. The selection included alligator, leather, patent leather, and everything else imaginable. Shiny boots were spotlighted along the back wall. He stopped at a pair of calf-high lace-ups similar to those he wore. His boots were old, and he admitted that it might be time to invest in a new pair. He looked at the price tag and coughed discretely.

Ravi laughed. *They will last you a lifetime, though. I can promise you that. Not everything more expensive is better, but this designer is worth the money. Those would look decent with your suit, too. I can't imagine you wearing dress shoes to kick ass anyway.*

Damian shrugged. *James Bond did.*

She chuckled. *Yeah, but 007 had a stunt double who* didn't *wear dress shoes.*

Good point. I can see myself slipping on a pile of ashes and sailing over the side of a building. I'd look good, but I'd be dead.

At least they wouldn't have to change you for burial.

The priest nodded. *True. That's convenient, I suppose.*

The demon squealed and Damian dropped the boot, looking around. *What? Where is it?*

She repeated the girlish shriek. *Do you see those leather heels on the showroom wall over there? Those are the same ones that Meghan, the Countess of Sussex, wore on one of her first outings with the prince before they were married. Oh, my gosh, they are so beautiful.*

Damian pursed his lips and bent to retrieve the boot. *I thought I had to slay a demon, and you're freaking out over heels?*

Ravi exhaled, awed. *There are so many beautiful shoes here. I would be in heaven if I could wear them.*

He tapped his foot. *I don't think my feet would fit in those. It might be a little unsightly, anyway, given the hair on the top of my feet.*

She giggled. *I don't know. I think those red pumps would be fantastic with your bowtie.*

The priest chuckled and rolled his eyes, thinking of Timothy's response. Ravi would love to be in his body. They would never shut up about fashion. Damian retreated and left the store without buying anything. They were at the end of the main shopping street, but he continued his stroll, enjoying the early evening air. He turned right at the end of the block, not sure where he was going.

A little farther down, he paused and studied a small sign pointing down an alley. "Huh. I wonder…"

He turned right and walked carefully down the clean walkway, finally reaching an iron gate. Cautiously, he pushed it open and looked around before stepping inside. A long stretch of bright green grass ahead was surrounded by trees, and a bench stood in the center. He had found one of the hidden Memorial Gardens that London was known for. Damian smiled. He hurried over, sat on the bench, and crossed his feet in front of him, enjoying the rest. As he soaked in the warmth of the sun, his phone rang.

The priest smiled as the Secretary's name appeared on the screen. He pressed Accept and put the phone to his ear. "Well, well, the stalker has returned. I knew you would miss me. Though I have to admit, it took you longer to call than I expected. You've perfected the whole make-him-think-you're-not-interested vibe. Good for you! I have a feeling you've had plenty of practice."

The Secretary's voice remained monotone. "Did you know that those Memorial Gardens have been there for over fifty years? The bench was added about twenty years ago, but it is very well-maintained. I especially like it during that time of year when the leaves on the trees turn from green to gold-yellows and burnt-oranges. If it weren't for you being there, it would be the perfect scenery."

Damian eyed the gold-yellow and burnt-orange leaves. He pursed his lips and shook his head as he sighed dramatically. "You are aware that stalking is illegal, right? Not that I could get a restraining order. You tend to stay well hidden. Or, like I said before, you *are* the drone, creeping up on me from afar. I knew that one day, technology would take over and try to kill us, but I didn't realize its personality would be so…English Nanny."

The Secretary smirked. "Well, when we first decided to take over the human race, we thought it would be a challenge. Then we realized how infantile you are, and we had to switch gears. It's easier to babysit than eliminate. We can have you do our bidding."

He shook his head. "So, the nanny cams are actually nannies."

"Yes, but we had to dumb them down so that people wouldn't want to play with them."

Damian laughed, finding the conversation amusing. It was the most the woman had ever said to him. She realized that too, and was quick to shut it down. "Moving on, I have a new assignment for you."

"Are you going to ask if I want it?"

The Secretary paused before answering, "No. You are to take Max with you as well. A spirit is wreaking havoc, damaging graves and scaring off mourners who come to the cemetery. He is a nasty bastard, and has perfected the art of launching objects into the air."

Damian groaned. "By objects do you mean rocks and stones, or are you talking about people? Dead or alive?"

She cleared her throat nervously. "Let's say we've had a few opened graves, several broken headstones, and at least one mausoleum moved about three hundred yards. The point is, he is completely out of hand. At first, it was a whisper of a haunting. Now, no one leaves unscathed. A large funeral was held there a week ago, with about three hundred mourners in attendance. The ghost appeared, chased them away, and started throwing people. At least a dozen were injured, and one was hung upside-down in a tree. It was the talk of the town. As you know, we don't smile on situations that turn into chatter amongst the townspeople."

He narrowed his eyes. "Do robots smile?"

The Secretary ignored him. "This cemetery is inside Castle Combe's grounds in the Cotswolds. It's one of England's prized historical sites, and the cemetery is the final resting place of some of the most prestigious artists and writers in our history. It is important that we attempt to preserve as much as possible when we deal with this ghost."

He snorted. "I like how you say 'we.' Where should I meet you to tackle this problem? I'm sure there is a charging station nearby for your battery."

The Secretary went quiet, and Damian laughed and slapped his hands on his lap. "I accept your mission, Secretary. Don't get any more uptight. You'll short a circuit."

"I suppose that might be better than getting my ass chewed by three old priests like you do on a regular basis simply by breathing," she snapped back.

Damian put his hand to his mouth. "Oooh, she's got jokes now. All right, bring it. Or should I say zero, one, one, zero, one, zero, one?"

The Secretary chuckled. "Let's try to take care of this ghost without knocking out any priests, innocents, or furry animals, shall we? I have complaints regarding the vehicles we send you. The companies are tired of cleaning blood, fur, and slobber from the carpets."

"Then you should probably groom a little better before you get into them."

A smile hovered on the priest's lips as her typing abruptly stopped. Finally, she said, "I'll send you the details. Don't fuck it up."

With that, she hung up. Damian placed the phone on the bench beside him and laughed, shaking his head. Ravi giggled. *One day, she will send us on a mission to the middle of Antarctica and leave us there.*

He waved his hands. *Nah, she likes us. I can tell. I think it's my fancy bowties.*

Just then, his phone buzzed again, and he squinted at the screen. The new text message from the Secretary wasn't her normal info drop. He opened it and read it out loud. "I would have to say that new suit suits you better than the hobo outfit you're wearing now."

The priest looked at his brown pants and button-up shirt and shook his head. "We need to carry an umbrella everywhere we go."

Ravi shrugged. *Maybe she likes the peepshow, or she likes to torture herself.*

CHAPTER SIX

Damian leaned against the doorframe of the upstairs training room and watched as Max completed the last ten of his fifty push-ups. Sweat beaded on the young man's forehead and his arms shook as he pushed his body up and lowered it to the floor. His face was the color of a tomato, but he was determined not to complain. "Forty-eight...forty-nine...fifty. Ugh."

He dropped to the floor and laid his cheek on the mat beneath him, breathing heavily. After a moment, he pushed up to his knees. Damian clapped and stretched to help him to his feet.

"That was impressive," his mentor said. "When you first came here, you could do six and a half."

Max shook his arms and lifted his eyebrows. "Yeah, that was definitely a challenge. What's next?"

Damian rubbed his hands together and bounced on the balls of his feet. "Let's work on our hand-to-hand combat skills, shall we? I will take offense, and you defend yourself. Imagine that my fingers have long, sharp talons."

The young priest squared his shoulders and stood eye to eye with his mentor. They circled one another, Damian's smile challenging. He faked with his left hand and swatted his adversary on the side of his head with his right. Max shook his head and quickly stiffened his arms. Damian feinted but didn't swing. Max lifted his hands and scowled because he'd fallen for it.

The older man chuckled. "The secret to defending yourself is anticipation." He swatted at the trainee, but Max knocked his hand away this time.

"The other secret is assuming that your opponent is smarter than you," Damian said.

He swept his foot, tripping Max, and knocked him twice on the back of the head. The trainee gritted his teeth and turned quickly, red flashing in his eyes. Damian immediately tapped him in the stomach and swatted his head again, chuckling.

"You can't let your frustration take over or you will have one hell of a headache tomorrow," he continued. "I know you're used to fighting bushes and all, but imagine you're fighting actual demons for a moment, okay?"

Damian threw his palms forward in a one-two combo. Max dodged clumsily and tripped over his own feet to fall on his ass with a grunt.

His mentor stopped and scrunched his forehead. "Maybe we should take a step back to not beating yourself up."

Max stood and put his hands up, trying to ignore the

smartass comments. Damian stood with his arms at his sides, watching him. Seconds later, he swung right and then left and boxed him in the ears without much effort.

Astaroth growled loudly. *Come on, can't you see him moving? You're like one of those rag dolls. You'd be better off dancing around him like a fool. It's all in reading the body. I've become somewhat of a pro at it. There! He's going to slap with his right.*

Max tried to shake the demon's voice out of his head, wanting to do it alone. Before he knew it, he received another slap. Astaroth sighed. *Now left. Damn. Now right. Come on, kid. Listen to me. You'll have little birdies flying around you for the next three days if you don't.*

I don't need help. I can do this.

Oh, sure. Go ahead then, Rambo. Show me what you got.

The young priest tried to dodge, but after a few more blows to his head, he began to see double. Damian didn't hurt him physically, but his pride was slowly being pulverized.

Astaroth whistled. *You had enough knocks to the dome? You ready to take my advice?*

Max groaned. *Fine.*

The demon studied Damian's moves and gave Max warning before each attack. Suddenly, Max was on a roll. He circled his opponent, dodging or blocking every blow. His mentor laughed loudly and picked up the pace. Still, with Astaroth in his ear, Max maintained his defense. He evaded the blows and slapped Damian's hands away. After the last attempt, the trainee stepped to the right, tapped Damian gently on the back of the head and chuckled.

The priest clapped and gave Max a knowing look. "One thing about having a demon is, there's no point in ignoring them. Sometimes they will save your life. Your moves are good, but you move your feet like Scooby Doo trying to run from a ghost. Make swift, short movements with your feet like you see in any boxing movie. It allows you to control your body better so if you face more than one foe, you can multitask. But let's leave that for another day. I don't need you to sprain an ankle."

Max looked at his feet and shrugged. "Yeah, probably a good choice."

Damian tossed him his towel and water bottle, and they caught their breath for a moment. They had worked out for almost two hours. It was something he'd promised would happen, not only for Max but for himself as well. He needed to stay nimble.

Max set his bottle down. "Did you guys train hard as mercs?"

"Every single day for hours and hours. We were badass. We had to be, though. It was what kept us alive. Come on, let's throw a few knives, then finish with a jog."

Max took his practice knives, looked at the dummy, and exhaled slowly. He reared back and threw, watching the weapon flip end over end. The blade struck the dummy's forehead.

Damian nodded his head, impressed. "You're getting that down. Now, work on speed. You want to throw at a second's notice and still be incredibly accurate."

The older priest turned abruptly and slapped the handle of a dagger on the table. He caught it deftly as it catapulted up and tossed it hard. The blade penetrated the head beside Max's knife, the metals scratching as they rubbed together.

The trainee's eyes widened, and he chuckled. "Well, that was pretty fucking cool."

Damian laughed, but in an instant, his head snapped toward his companion. "Language."

Max's shoulders dropped, and he attempted the same thing Damian had done. He managed to catch the knife, but when he threw, it slammed sideways into the target and clanged to the floor.

His mentor raised an eyebrow. "Well, good to know that if we face any midget demons, you got it on lock. This isn't one of those 'go for the knees' scenarios."

Max rolled his eyes and scrunched his nose. "Yeah, I'll leave you with the theatrics."

Damian patted him on the shoulder. "Probably a good choice. Come on. Twenty minutes on the treadmill."

Max hopped wearily onto one of the treadmills. They set the timers and adjusted the incline to fifty percent. As they began to run, he leaned his forearms on the railings and looked at his feet. "Any news on the home front?"

Damian nodded his head, breathing heavily. "Actually, I was about to tell you. The Secretary called, and we have a new mission. We head out after dinner. There is a spirit in the cemetery near Castle Combe. He's apparently a real jerk, and we need to go in and exorcise him. Of course, we've been asked to do it with as little damage as possible."

Max chuckled. "Right. Will there be any demons out there, or is this simply a haunting?"

"I don't know," Damian replied. "It's probably only the ghost, but we'll go prepared just in case. I hope it's an easy spirit to vanquish, and we can grab some coffee and come home."

The young priest wiped the sweat from his forehead with the back of his arm. "Well, that means there will probably be eleven ghosts and forty demons on site."

Damian laughed. "You're catching on, kid."

They finished their run and headed to their rooms to shower and change. Max joined Damian in the kitchen, rubbing a towel over his hair. "What's for dinner? I'm starving."

The older man turned the stove off and served the pasta on two plates. "We had some leftover pasta from the other night, so I warmed that up, and there's garlic bread and wine on the table."

Max grabbed two glasses, and they sat opposite one another in the dining room. Damian set up his tablet and opened the map of the cemetery the Secretary had sent. He explained the plan of attack he'd formulated as they ate.

He pointed to the center of the cemetery. "So, because it's outside, the heart is pretty much anywhere. This ghost likes to torment mourners. The plan is for you to go in dressed in street clothes and pick one of the headstones around this area. You make like you're praying and wait for the ghost to manifest. From the video footage they sent over, this spirit doesn't leave any mourner untouched. It shouldn't take long for him to appear. Once he's in the open, I'll start the exorcism and you will join me."

Max swallowed a mouthful of pasta and took a gulp of

his wine. "This plan sounded good until I became the dangling meat."

His mentor smirked. "Somebody's gotta be the bait, brother. You are younger."

"Great, and I may never see old age."

Damian smiled and pointed to the entrance of the cemetery. "You'll walk in through here as if to visit. I'll scoot in from the side entrance and hide until he comes out. There are three large tombs here, and you want to stay far from those. Don't give him an excuse to use them as weapons. To the left is the rubble pile the crew created from the destroyed headstones. We'll keep our distance from that, too."

Max's eyes widened, and he nodded. "I definitely don't want Noble Jones's headstone becoming my own in the middle of a dark cemetery. I want to be cremated anyway."

"Well, that happens from time to time for us Damned, even when we don't plan for it."

Max curled his lip, remembering the ash piles. "Oh, yeah. Maybe I'll go with a mausoleum instead."

After the meal, the trainee washed the dishes and put them away. He met Damian in the garage, and they packed their bags with guns, knives, bibles, and their crosses. Max pulled his sash out, but Damian put his hand up and shook his head. "You can't wear your uniform. You gotta wear street clothes. You got any?"

"Yeah. Completely forgot. I'll be right back."

Damian pulled his gloves on and grasped his special metal cross. He had used it many times but hadn't noticed how light it was until that moment. It weighed little more than a plastic one, and he wondered if it had always been that way.

It has, Ravi replied. *You grip it so tightly that you don't really notice.*

He shrugged and slipped it into the inside leather pocket of his jacket. *Nice. I might be able to use that as leverage for something.*

The door creaking brought his attention to Max. Damian did a double-take, barely recognizing the young priest. He wore a pair of jeans, Chuck Taylors, a green t-shirt, and a blue V-neck sweater. His hands were stuffed nervously into his pockets as he stepped into the garage.

Ravi whistled loudly in Damian's head. *What the ever-loving fuck? How have I lived in the same house as this guy and not known how stinking hot he is? That youth is wasted on the uniform, I'm telling you. He is a fucking heartthrob. Jesus.*

He handed Max his belt, trying to maintain his nonchalance. *Can you please keep your howling and drooling to yourself? It's really weird to have a voice in my head turned on by another guy, not to mention that he's a priest.*

The demon sighed. *It's not like there's a ton of eye candy around here for me on a regular basis. I got you, which is a big no. And Rose, the old-ass woman across the street.*

Damian zipped his bag with a frown. *Are you telling me you swing both ways?*

Ravi scoffed. *I don't discriminate. How about them apples, man of God? Not only do you have a demon in you, but she likes the Vajayjay and the Cock-a-doodle-doo. It's like a triple sin in here.*

He chuckled.

Max looked up and smiled. "What?"

Damian shook his head. "Nothing. Revelations are sprouting all over the place these days. I'm starting to think retirement is calling my name."

The trainee closed the doors to the SUV. "Pfft. Yeah, right. You'll be fucking demons up from your scooter when your legs give out. Your twenty-one-gun salute will be aimed at a portal spilling demons."

His mentor laughed loudly. "Damn fucking straight."

CHAPTER SEVEN

Castle Combe was one of the oldest towns in England, dating back to the twelfth century. The village took its name from the fortress that stood in ruin and rubble on the outskirts. The cemetery on the grounds was still used, and tombs of unknown villagers and noblemen sprawled on the hill overlooking the town below. Over time small tombs and mausoleums had been added, along with tall, looming angel statues guarding the interred dead.

Damian and Max waited to the right of the cemetery within the thin forest. The older priest studied the area but saw no movement in the moonlight. He turned to the trainee and slapped him on the chest. "All right, buddy. You ready for this?"

Max nodded somberly. "You know me—I walk right into the middle of the fire without a care in the world."

Damian didn't pay attention to his sarcasm. "That's my

boy. I'll have my eyes on you the whole time, so go get him. Hopefully, we can be in and out of here in a jiffy."

Max took a deep breath, shoved his bible into the back of his pants, and pulled his sweater over it. "Here goes nothing."

He took a deep breath, thrust his hands into his pockets, and walked out onto the gravel road. At the gate, he paused, his eyes noting the specific tombs and statues that would lead him to the heart of the cemetery. He whistled as he walked past rows of tombstones adorned with flowers and wreaths. When he reached the center, his eyes focused on one of the newer stones. The name read Betty Alderson, and he dropped to one knee and ran his hand across the text. He bowed his head, pretending prayer, but remained alert for any sign of the ghost.

Several silent moments passed, disturbed only by the wind whipping through the trees. Suddenly, Max heard a low, deep laugh roll across the stones to his left. He lifted his head as the shadowy shape of an apparition darted forward and rose above the headstone before him. Max swallowed hard as the ghost took form. He was a tall, slender man in a dress coat and white shirt. His stovepipe hat seemed incongruous perched above a face of rotting flesh and bone.

The young priest took a step back, his heart beating fast in his chest. He slid his hand slowly behind him and beneath his sweater for his bible. Damian would be there soon, but he was prepared to exorcise the evil spirit if he needed to. The ghost twisted his head to the side and grinned from ear to ear. Most of his teeth were missing or chipped. Max mumbled under his breath, "Any time now, Damian."

His mentor stepped from the shadows of the mausoleum, holding his cross in the air. His bible was open in front of him, but he didn't need to look at the words. Max released a slow breath of relief. The ghost twisted, following his gaze. As soon as he saw Damian, he screeched loudly and formed his translucent bony hands into fists.

He was more than pissed. "You tricked me."

Damian smirked. "That's right, asshole. It's time to move on."

The spirit laughed loudly and swirled, floating into the air. His ghostly body swerved to the right and yanked a headstone from the ground. Max's eyes widened as the entity threw the stone at him. Dirt and grass flew everywhere as he dived out of the way and slid across the wet earth. The ghost drifted to the rubble at the back of the cemetery. Boulders and debris, remnants of the castle the Normans had built centuries before, had been piled high.

One after another, the ghost threw these missiles at the two men, crushing any headstones in the way. Max ran toward the side of the cemetery and leaped forward as a boulder barely missed him. He tucked and rolled across the grass, landing on his stomach. Moving instinctively, he scrambled to shelter behind a medium-sized tomb. The sound of stone shattering echoed violently.

Max drew his legs to his chest and leaned against the cold tomb's wall. He ducked as a piece of debris struck the top and crumbled over him, and covered his mouth with his hand, trying not to cough. He searched for Damian, but he was nowhere in sight. Max closed his eyes, growling his irritation. He crawled the length of the tomb and peered around the corner. He snapped his head back as a tombstone narrowly missed him.

He breathed deeply, pressed himself against the stone wall, and whispered a prayer of protection under his breath. "God, protect me from this scary ghost. Let us get through this in one solid, living piece."

Astaroth chuckled. *That's one hell of a prayer, kid. You think He's actually listening?*

Max whimpered slightly and nodded. *He's always listening. At least, that's what they tell me. I'm not sure if He'll find this the right time to do anything about it, but it never hurts to ask.*

The demon laughed louder. *Actually, sometimes it does. I don't know how happy He will be with the desecration of a holy cemetery, but hey, maybe I'm wrong.*

The young priest groaned and ran his hands over his face and through his hair. He crawled to the opposite side, looking for Damian, but another tomb blocked his view. *I gotta find Damian. I gotta know what the plan is when everything goes to shit. God will protect me. I know it. God will.*

Right then, a metal pole erupted from the wall beside his head. He froze and stared at the skull dangling from the end of the rod. His own blood-curdling and deafening scream shocked him into action. He swatted at the skull until it fell and rolled across the ground.

Astaroth grimaced. *I had no idea your voice could reach that octave.*

Max breathed heavily, kicking the head farther away.

Really? I did. I'm pretty sure that was the same scream I gave when I was thirteen and saw a demon for the first time.

And how did that work out for you?

He shrugged. *He chased me down a dark alley. I only got away because there was a street full of people on the other side.*

Astaroth groaned. *Okay, little girl, get your shit together. You can't hide here all night. You need to either find Damian or get this exorcism over with on your own. I don't think you're ready for it, so your best bet is to find the chief.*

Max nodded wildly. *Yeah, I'll find Damian.*

He swallowed hard and crawled beneath the pole and beyond the tomb. From there, he stayed low, army-crawling between headstones. When he made it to an angel statue, he pressed his back against its square base to catch his breath. He glanced back at the tomb he had left as the roof caved in and the walls tumbled. "That could have been bad."

Astaroth barked at him, *It still can, sissy pants. Get your ass in gear and find Damian.*

Max nodded. *Right. Going.*

He resumed his crawl, peeking occasionally over the tops of the tombstones, and finally spotted his mentor standing in the open. He exhaled a nervous breath, glad to see the priest was still alive and in one piece, then continued across the graves. Every time his hands and knees touched another burial surface, he had to resist the urge to make the sign of the cross. It felt terrible to scramble over people's final resting places.

Astaroth was about to kill the kid. *They are dead. I promise you they aren't mad at you for this. Keep going before you don't have a chest to cross.*

Max was closer to Damian now, and the ghost was swirling around the cemetery in the background. The spirit shrieked and screamed, seeking anything he could throw.

Damian gripped his bible tightly in one hand and the cross in the other as he took another step forward. He shouted the words of a very long exorcism, knowing he needed something with some oomph to eliminate an entity that strong. *"Exorcizo te, omnis spiritus immunde, in nomine Dei, Patris Omnipotentis…"* His eyes shifted to follow the streaks of light that trailed the spirit through the cemetery. He growled and dropped his hands, knowing he wasn't close enough for his prayer to have an impact. For now, the ghost was pissed and too busy searching for Max to pay him any attention. He shook his head and raised his arms, ready to start again. Eventually, he would get the asshole's attention.

Before he could speak, though, he heard a whisper behind him. "Psst. Damian. Hey."

He looked over his shoulder at Max, who was hiding behind a statue of the Angel Michael. Damian waved him closer. "Get out here."

The young man nodded wildly and hurried to him, still hunched over. "Sorry. I had to find you."

Damian stared at his companion. "Was that you screaming or a cat dying?"

Max rubbed his hand through his hair and slumped. "I mean, it could have been either. I'm sure there are a ton of stray cats out here."

The older priest's lips twitched. "You sounded like a little girl."

"What? The skull of the dead person from that tomb popped out right near my face. If that were you, I promise you would have screamed too. A metal pole almost took my head off at the same time."

Damian grabbed him by the shirt collar and thrust him forward. "Go to the center and lure that bastard back here. I can't exorcise him if he is all over the place. He needs to be here. Go. I'm right behind you with the bible and the cross."

Max looked at him with pursed lips, wanting to argue but knowing the older priest was right. He turned toward the center of the cemetery, which was only fifty feet in front of him. In the distance, the ghost yelled loudly and yanked an entire casket from the ground. He threw it hard and it crashed into the dirt, spilling bones and jewelry. Max almost turned back, but breathed deeply and closed his eyes as he straightened slowly. The spirit didn't see him, so he cupped his mouth and yelled, "Hey, fucker! You looking for me?"

The spectral head swiveled, and he dropped the skull he held. He smirked viciously and raced across the cemetery, stopping barely twenty-five feet from the young priest. As the entity swirled in circles around him, Max stiffened his shoulders, trying to control his breathing. In reality, he was utterly terrified and didn't know what to expect. What he *did* know was this was his life now, and he had to get his brave on in these situations. Damian had told him before that he would be no good to anyone if he couldn't keep his head. It was hard, though, with that thing circling closer and closer.

Damian intoned the exorcism as the spirit whipped

around his prey like a cyclone. The older priest walked forward slowly, fighting the wind. He held his cross high as he spoke with intensity and feeling. With every step closer, the ghost faltered. He put his hands to his ears and screamed to scare them. Still, Damian moved relentlessly forward.

After about two minutes, the wraith froze and began to shake violently. The wind increased as he rose into the air. Damian stopped the prayer and bolted toward Max. He grabbed him by the shoulders and yanked him behind a pile of rubble. The young man nodded in thanks, and Damian patted his shoulder. "This one might be messy."

They turned, gripped the stone at the top, and peeked over. The entity twisted and writhed, his face fading in and out. Suddenly, he spun sharply and thrust his arm into the air. His spine-chilling voice echoed across the cemetery. "He shall find you, and when he does, all of the fallen will gather at your doorstep."

Max looked at Damian, who narrowed his eyes. The older priest had no idea what that meant, but it sounded important. With everything regarding Lilith and the cardinal going on, he had a hard time believing it didn't correlate in some way. Before he could really consider that, the ghost began to glow vividly. Damian pulled Max to the ground, and they huddled together as the entity flared into unnatural brightness before exploding.

Black goo spattered in all directions and coated the grass, narrowly missing the two men. Max wrinkled his nose and put his face in his arm. "Holy ghost hell, that dude smells terrible."

"How do you think *you* would smell after a century without a shower?"

They stood and gazed at the destruction. The place was a wreck, but they had managed to fulfill the most important part of the mission. Damian patted Max's shoulder. "Let's get a drink."

CHAPTER EIGHT

They found a small pub in the village for drinks before returning home. Max ordered a beer and two shots to calm himself. Ravi pouted when Damian opted for beer instead of whiskey. He had a long drive ahead, and was already exhausted from the day.

The older priest leaned back in his chair and took a sip. After swallowing, he shook his head and laughed. "Oh, man. Seriously, that was crazy."

Max chuckled and downed his shot. "Yeah, so much for keeping the destruction to a minimum."

"It wasn't pretty, but we're both still alive. The restless spirit is at peace now, and so are we." Damian savored a mouthful of beer. "There's nothing quite like a good ale after a near-death experience."

"Near-death?" Max asked. "I thought we had the situation well in hand."

His mentor laughed easily. "Yes, from the sound of your girlish screams, you clearly weren't worried at all."

"Will I ever hear the end of that?" the trainee asked and looked dejectedly at his beer.

"Not until the end of this meal, at the very least."

"Then hurry up and finish that steak, old man."

"You know, other than your panicked shrieks—"

"I did *not* shriek," Max protested.

Damian gave him a flat look. "I suspect once the rumors of the ghost die down, the townspeople will talk about the screaming banshee of Castle Combe cemetery for years to come."

"All I hear is that my actions tonight will live on in local legend," Max retorted.

His mentor laughed and shook his head. "I wanted to say you did well tonight, but I don't know if your ego can handle another compliment. Pride is a sin, after all."

"You really think so?" Max asked. "You think I did well?"

Damian took a sip of his beer and nodded. "You moved fast, you deliberately put yourself in danger to accomplish the mission, and you came back for me when you couldn't find me. Those are excellent traits in a teammate. Good job."

Max's smile slowly widened. "Thanks. I'll admit it cost me to be brave out there, but I knew I had to. It was you and me, and you couldn't do it on your own."

"I'll drink to that." Damian lifted his pint glass, his companion clinked it with his, and they drank in cheerful silence.

Max wiped his mouth with a napkin and looked at Damian. "What did the ghost mean before he exploded? He said something like, 'he shall find you, and the fallen will gather at your doorstep?' What does that mean?"

Damian glanced at him and forced a smile. He didn't want the young priest to know that he had his suspicions about what the ghost meant. "Who the hell knows? When I was a merc, demons said wild shit all the time, and no one knew what it meant. It was either random and cryptic or in a language we didn't speak. I learned not to waste brain-power worrying about it."

Max eyed him for a moment and nodded in under-standing. "So, what do mercs do all day? I know what they do when they're called out, but what about the rest of the time? And why did you decide to come back to work for the church? From what I heard, it was a pretty good gig working for the Killers. Good money, no lack of adventure, comradery, and family you wouldn't find anywhere else. I don't get why you would give that up to deal with the BS you deal with from the Wise Men."

The waitress refilled their water glasses. Damian swal-lowed and thanked her, waiting for her to leave before he spoke. He knew mercs weren't secret anymore, but he still felt strange talking about it in the open where anyone could hear.

He took a sip of his beer and put the glass down, then leaned forward and lowered his voice. "Being a merc now is different. Before Incursion Day, we stayed at the base, hung out together, trained several times a day, and chilled. We went out to different places, but we couldn't have bank accounts or anything."

Max looked confused. "Why?"

Damian smiled. "Well, before Incursion Day, being

Damned gave you three choices. You could choose death, become a test subject, or join the mercs. There was no government division yet, and if you chose merc, you immediately died to your old life. They would literally bury an empty casket and mourn with your family. So we could go do stuff, but we had to be careful who we ran into. There was a real line there. After Incursion Day, everything changed. You didn't have to join the mercs or the government. You could go rogue, or you no longer had to fight demons, even if you were Damned."

Max nodded. "That's how I thought it was, though I was pretty sure if you were Damned and unaffiliated, you ran the risk of being killed out in the world."

The priest sighed. "Unfortunately, that's true. The mercs have changed, though. They work with the government, have lives, homes, and families, and are less constrained. As for why I came back to the church...well, I had never really left. I worked for the church with the mercs, and when the opportunity for this assignment came, I prayed about it and felt God was leading me back to the church fulltime to save lost souls."

Max thought about it for a second and smiled. "Wow, you really *have* been through a lot. Have you ever reached a point where you'd rather kill the demon than exorcise it?"

Damian gulped his beer, his gaze shifting to the other patrons. His thoughts wandered back ten years to the battle at the amusement park. He could almost feel the rage that had built in him that night. Max was waiting for an answer and Damian forced a crooked smile.

He wanted to give his assistant the truth but not scare him with his story. "Everyone reaches breaking points throughout their lives. That's a reality. I have seen things that will never be erased from my memory. But the truth I always hold onto is that when I'm weak, the church reminds me of why I need to be strong. My vows remind me why I need to do it the right way. Without that, we would all succumb to our human instinct for revenge."

The two fell silent, sipping their beers, lost in their own thoughts. Damian recalled all the times he'd pulled the trigger when he should have opened the bible.

Max considered the future and how he would handle death and heartbreak in the days to come. Would he succumb to the need for revenge, or would he put his faith in the church? Only time would tell, and he hoped he had plenty of that left.

Damian finished the last of his beer and set the glass down briskly. "You ready?"

Max nodded and gulped the last drops in his glass. "Yeah. We have a long ride back. Thanks, man."

The older man signaled for the waitress and handed her his card. "No problem. I'll make sure to put down another favor owed."

"Great. You should give me the choice on these, though."

Damian chuckled and signed the receipt. They shuffled out to the SUV and Max looked at Damian, who yawned widely. "You want me to drive?"

"After two shots? Nah, I got this. But thanks, I appreciate it. Sit back and relax."

Max leaned his head back and stared out the window. Damian gripped the steering wheel tightly and accelerated slowly down the cobblestone streets. As they left Castle

Combe and turned onto the main road, his phone vibrated in his pocket. He retrieved it, rolling his eyes at the Secretary's name on the screen. He knew the call wasn't to tell them they'd done a good job. Still, he had no other option but to answer.

It was the part of his new job he hated most. As a merc, he didn't answer to anyone but Korbin, and even when the church did call, they rarely gave criticism or orders. That freedom for all those years had been good. He shrugged, accepting that he had to trade something to do what he felt called to do. Max looked at him, and he showed him the name. "Duty calls, as usual. I can't even take a nice quiet car ride for five minutes. I guess I should have expected it. She knows when I'm sleeping and when I'm awake."

The trainee raised an eyebrow. "The Secretary is Santa Claus?"

"Not even close to being that jolly." Damian pressed the Answer button with a huge grin. "Good to hear from you, Secretary. I assume you're calling to tell me how well Max and I did at the cemetery? It means a lot to me that you took the time to call, but you didn't have to do so this late."

She coughed lightly. "It amazes me that I order you not to destroy, and yet you leave chaos in your wake wherever you go. I did consider switching it up and telling you to go nuts but decided reverse psychology would be wasted on you. I'd be left holding the bag for the fireball from hell you unleashed."

Damian smirked. "Glad you liked our work. Next time, maybe expect less when a giant ghost throws caskets full of bones at our heads. Mm-kay? Great. Thanks for the consideration."

The Secretary sighed. "As much as I love to go back and forth with you, that's not why I'm calling. I need you to take a detour—the next exit coming up."

He looked at the sign as they passed it and eased his foot off the gas to slow as they approached the ramp. "You know, I told myself today that maybe it's good she always knows where I am. Then I thought, yeah, sure. I've always wanted someone looking over my shoulder every second of the day. I always wanted an extra pair of eyes when I take a shower to make sure I reached all the spots on my back. You know, those hard-to-reach places."

Damian took the exit and pulled off on the side of the road. He flipped the overhead light on and tapped his fingers on the steering wheel. "Okay, boss. I've taken the exit. What would you like me to do?"

The Secretary typed quickly, the noise clicking in his ear. "Hold on one second. I'm sending it to you."

Suddenly, the GPS turned on, and a thin red line trailed across the map on the screen. Damian tapped it with his finger and narrowed his eyes. "That's fucking weird. I won't lie. This shit borders on apocalyptic."

She exhaled a sharp breath. "Seriously? You fight demons trying to take over the world and worry that I can turn your GPS on from here? Perhaps you should rethink the priorities here. Besides, your car is ours. Of course, I can control certain things from here. Trust me, it's not magic. I don't have a cauldron and a wand. A voodoo doll, maybe, but a wand, no."

"I thought my back pain was worse than normal."

"Mmm. And don't worry. Tonight, the pain will move to another spot. Your legs and kneecaps are still in perfect condition. I'll make sure to remedy that with some pins and a bottle of wine."

Damian wasn't entirely sure she was joking, so he opted for the directions. "So, Voodoo Queen, where am I going?"

The Secretary chuckled. "A village fifty miles away. There is a church in the center of the town. Don't worry, this place is teeny-tiny, and there is only one church. The three Wise Men are already waiting for you at the side entrance."

He slouched and groaned loudly. "God, what did I do now?"

She cleared her throat. "You don't have to call me God. 'Secretary' will suffice. And nothing that I know of, but you have fifty miles to go, so anything can happen."

Damian shook his head firmly. "Nope. Not tonight. I won't veer from this path. It will be an unexciting fifty-mile drive."

"Good to know. I believe they have something to discuss with you about another mission they want you to go on. This one is pretty hush-hush, and they said you have to know before I'm briefed. I wish I could tell you more. Actually no, I lie. I like to see you sweat."

"Very funny. All right, we're on our way. At this time of night, it shouldn't take more than an hour and a half or so to get there."

The Secretary was about to hang up when she remembered something. "Oh, and don't forget, leave Max in the car. You know how the Wise Men are about that. They don't want him in the meetings yet."

Damian sneered. "Lucky bastard."

She stifled a laugh. "Have fun. And please hide those bags of guns. You know what will happen if they see them."

The priest looked into the rearview mirror at the two duffel bags tucked in the dark corner. He was about to ask her how she knew when the line clicked. He dropped the phone in the cupholder.

Max raised an eyebrow. "New mission?"

Damian sighed. "Not yet, but soon. The Wise Men want to talk to me about it in person in a small town about fifty miles from here."

Max straightened and brushed imaginary crumbs from the front of his shirt. "Oh, I didn't realize we were meeting them."

He shook his head. "No worries. They aren't ready for you to join the party. Yet again, you have been blessed by Lady Luck. You get to sit in the car and wait for me to come back with half my dignity intact."

The young priest chuckled. "Don't worry, you always walk around like that."

Damian shot him a dirty look and smirked as they drove on in silence.

CHAPTER NINE

The SUV moved slowly through the small village. The cobblestone streets were so narrow that Damian wondered if he should even drive on them. The village was so small that it seemed stuck in the past, and the two priests looked at the few people who were still out as they passed them. While some appeared normal, others were dressed as they would have been a hundred years earlier.

To Damian, the place was eerie. Old stone houses, some with thatched roofs, lined the roads.

Max leaned his head against the cold glass and smiled. "I like this village. It's quaint and quiet. I half expect everything to be lantern-lit. From the looks of the crap piles on the street, it doesn't seem like they drive anything but horses, either. It's homey and warm, which is what I miss most about being human."

Ravi scoffed. *Are you kidding me? If I want to immerse myself in the past, I'll turn on the goddamned History Channel. This place is creepy as fuck. I half-expect these villagers to have red eyes, torches, and pitchforks. I want to go home to our chair by the fireplace.*

Damian glanced at the church ahead. *Trust me, you're not alone. I want to go home too. Unfortunately, the triplets want to see me, and I have to oblige.*

The demon growled. *I don't understand why you put up with them. Seriously, you have worked for the church for decades.*

Think of it this way. People work for companies for thirty or thirty-five years before retiring. Do you think that because they worked there for so long, they disrespect their bosses?

Well...no.

He nodded. *These guys are my bosses so I won't pick a fight with them. They are the soothsayers, the healers, and the men of God I answer to. Let's get through it and move on from there.*

Ravi groaned. *Fine, but make this fast and furious, please. I don't feel like tea and crumpets with those creepy-ass guys.*

Not a problem. I feel the same way. Hopefully, we're in and out. These guys don't want to hang out with me any more than I want to be there.

Damian braked sharply as a dog ran across the street. The priests exchanged bemused glances as they edged forward slowly and stopped two blocks up in front of the small white church. Max couldn't imagine it holding more than thirty people, but then the village probably had less than three hundred residents.

The windshield fogged slightly in the cold late-night air. Max turned his head and huffed. "Are you sure I can't tag along? I mean, what would they do if I came in with you? Would they refuse to give you the new assignment?"

Damian snorted. "Probably. They are some of the most

stubborn people I've ever met, stuck in the old church ways. They tend to frown on our new and lively ways of doing things. To be honest, they would probably kick you out. Once you stand in front of them, I promise you wouldn't fight them. They may be old, but they're intimidating."

Max folded his arms and pouted. "You leave me out of things wherever we go. First the Wally thing, then those books you read. This is simply another moment where I'm pushed aside."

The older priest shrugged into his jacket. "Remember, this isn't on me. I don't make the rules or decisions for these men. I know what is required, and I obey. Right now, the standing order is that Max doesn't sit with the Wise Men yet. Anyway, I don't know why you're so upset. I'm dead serious when I say that you're lucky to be excluded. They're not the most exciting people and are known to be bullies. Besides, do you want to meet them in a dirty pair of jeans and a sweater?"

The trainee scowled at his clothes and brushed at a stray twig. "I suppose you're right, at least on that. I feel strange out of my uniform. I haven't worn civilian clothes in ages, and wasn't even sure they would fit."

Damian smiled as he removed his cross from his jacket pocket and stuck it carefully behind the seat. He knew that arming himself would make the Wise Men nervous, and that wasn't what he wanted to do. He retained only his bible; it would be a mistake to not bring it into the meeting. He had done that once a long time before, and it ended in a three-hour lecture of how the church fathers should always have bibles in hand.

Max finally relented but huffed as he plopped back in his seat. Damian smiled broadly and stepped onto the sidewalk, depressed the lock button, and closed the door. He could feel Max's gaze as he hurried up the eight steps to the entrance. The doors were locked. Damian groaned and headed back down the steps and turned toward the rear of the building.

He stepped over a large puddle and grumbled. *Of course, they have to meet in the dungeon. I don't think I've ever seen any of them out and about in the air.*

Ravi giggled. *Maybe they are the reality of Twilight. Like middle-aged Twilight.*

Damian tried to hold the laughter back by pressing his lips together. *That would definitely not be a winner at the box office.*

The demon sighed as they approached the basement door. *I don't get it. Those three are fucking creepy. I feel like they lurk in dark basements having circle jerks and deciding who is the toughest. When no one is around, they sit around barechested like Russian fighters.*

His laughter erupted, stopping him in his tracks. He drew a breath, pushed the amusement down, and reminded himself that those men were his bosses. Despite what he thought, he had to at least attempt to act professionally. Damian squared his shoulders and descended the staircase. He entered the narrow door and let it shut behind him before starting down the long hall. At the first doorway, he poked his head around the corner and smiled.

The three Wise Men sat at a large wooden table, dressed in their normal black robes. Damian cleared his throat nervously and stepped inside, clasping his hands in front of him. He quickly took a seat in the empty chair in front of them, not sure if he should speak first.

In the short silence that followed, he looked from one priest to the next. They were not at all fazed by his arrival. Ravi coughed. *Okay, this is like a stare showdown. Why does it have to be in some creepy-ass basement? And why do they get robes? I want to wear a robe everywhere.*

Damian slowed his breathing and clasped his hands in his lap. *Me too, Ravi. Me too. We could have it made from the same material as that shirt-tent thing you had me try on. It could be a cape and a rain jacket. Boom. Multitasking.*

The demon laughed. *I think you might be onto something there. They could become all the rage for creepy priests, super-heroes, and the weird guy who likes to wear one around the house with nothing but his underwear.*

Before Damian could respond, Father Judah cleared his throat, catching his attention. "Damian, thank you for making a detour to meet us. We know your schedule is usually busy, but we believe this is of grave importance."

Father Christoff spoke next, tapping his fingers on the table beneath the long sleeves of his robes. "You did a good job dispatching that ghost to the next life. The people of Castle Combe will be very grateful that they can once again visit the graves of their loved ones without being tormented or injured, though I must point out that again you did little to preserve the historic surroundings."

Damian lifted a finger and opened his mouth, ready to defend himself. The spirit was responsible for the destruction, not him and Max. He wasn't sure it was the right time or setting to protest, though, so he lowered his hand and waited. It was best to take their thanks and act dumb.

Ravi sniffed. *I wonder what they hide in there?*

He glanced at the robes. *Probably snacks, a Gutenberg Bible, and extra robes. You know, the normal stuff.*

Yeah, right. They probably have at least a dozen choir boys, the souls of redheaded children, and a Cerberus in their pocket.

Damian managed to keep a straight face. *And a Cup of Noodles in their left pocket. You know, in case hunger strikes in an inopportune basement or shadowy parking lot.*

I wonder if they carry vampire spray and garlic with them? By day, they are the Wise Men. By night, they are the three vampire-slaying babes of Orange County.

His lips twitched as he struggled to hold back the laugh. *Knock it off if you want to get out of here soon.*

Father Judah slid a folder across the table. Damian took it and opened it to a page that seemed to be about Scotland. "Am I going on some sort of vacation?"

The wise man smirked. "No, but we do have a new mission for you. This one is top secret, and you are the first to know about it outside our circle. Even the Secretary won't be briefed before you are. I hope you understand the need to keep these things secret. The public has suffered enough anguish in this war. If we can maintain silence and deal with it, there is no reason to incite any more fear."

Damian nodded. "I agree. On top of that, people often get injured trying to be heroes in a situation they don't fully understand."

Father Judah nodded. "I agree. We want to keep the casualties to a minimum, and it's encouraging that you're on the same page as us. You'll be able to tell Max, of course, but that's it. On that note, let's talk specifics."

Damian looked at the file as Father Judah spoke in a

low, steady tone. "Your destination is Scotland, but the exact location is not important at this moment. A large group of infected worshipers is wreaking havoc there. The demons grab the innocent, infect them, and either force them into this ragtag army or sacrifice them to the demon leader, Moloch. From what I've heard, that is not a new name to you."

The priest snorted and shook his head. "No, Father. He caused trouble for my old team and continues to do so on a regular basis. Will there be mercenaries present as well?"

Father Christoff nodded but gave a loud grunt of derision. "We don't like to involve them, but this is a massive scene, so yes. We're not sure which ones, but they'll expect you and Max. They know your main objective is to exorcise, but I can't promise they will respect that."

"Not to worry. I have more than enough experience with mercs to deal with this."

Father Judah provided more details as Damian leaned back in his chair and flipped through the file. A glance at the three priests revealed faces devoid of expression. They always looked serious and worried, and it creeped him out. Not only had these men been with the church for a very long time, but they also kept secrets. The things they had seen over the years were preserved inside them, locked away from the world.

Damian rubbed his chin as the entry from the journal came to mind. The cardinal had spent a lot of time with the Wise Men in the past—even in the recent past. Damian knew that they knew more about the missing priest than met the eye, and it took everything in him to focus his attention on Father Judah. He wanted to find the cardinal because he could feel in the pit of his stomach that the man was involved in the chaos around them. Asking this team, though, would only cause problems.

Ravi clicked her tongue, bored. *Why do they act all cryptic about this shit? I mean, seriously, it's an incursion. They happen like every other day now. These guys watch way too many dramas on television. Just send us out there so we can start kicking some fucking ass already.*

He glanced at Father Christoff, who was staring daggers at him. He knew he couldn't see him talking to Ravi, but it was like he harbored some personal vendetta—and for all Damian knew, the other fathers were in on it too. He merely had to figure out exactly what *it* was.

CHAPTER TEN

Damian closed the file and focused his attention on Father Judah so he could ignore the stares of the other two. "So, we go to this undisclosed location and exorcise as many demons as possible while cooperating as best we can with the mercs on the scene?"

Father Judah nodded his head. "Yes, precisely. We need you to leave tomorrow. Of course, return to London first, rest today, and pack for the trip. When you leave here, I will brief the Secretary. She will make all the arrangements and contact you with that information as soon as it is available."

Damian chewed the inside of his cheek as Father Christoff released another snort of derision. "Make sure you keep Max safe. There will be many demons, and a significant number won't have human bodies to exorcise."

"At the same time," Father Judah added, "we believe this would be a very good time for him to be fully involved in exorcisms on site."

Damian frowned. "We are already at that point. He is involved in every case. I stand with him and make sure that he executes the correct sequence of prayers and understands the risks involved."

Father Judah glanced at his colleagues. "I don't think you fully understand. We want him on the ground doing his own work. Think of him as your partner in this upcoming assignment rather than your trainee."

He was slightly taken back. "With all due respect, Fathers, Max has only been on a handful of assignments. He's not ready to handle a situation of this magnitude on his own. He has never been involved with anything this large. He has no idea how the mercs work and isn't physically prepared to fight demons off with no protection. The best thing for his safety is to keep him close and help him through it. By assisting me, he learns valuable lessons each time we work. What you suggest would bring undue stress and possibly cause serious injury, if not death."

Father Christoff leaned forward. "You won't let that happen. You will allow him to work on his own while keeping an eye on him at all times. This is what we believe is best at this point."

Damian balled his fist in his lap. "I am only one man. Watching him from a distance will leave me open to attacks. This is highly irregular, and I don't believe—"

"It is not up for discussion," Father Judah interrupted. "Full exorcisms during the incursion. Are you able to do this or do we need to transfer him to someone more capable?"

He gritted his teeth and nodded, knowing there was no point in a continued argument. Father Judah nodded happily and retrieved the file. "Then we look forward to hearing your report when you both return. Good luck, and may God be with you."

Damian stood and bowed his head. "And with you, Fathers."

He shuffled awkwardly out the doorway and down the hall, his teeth clenched tightly and his fists balled at his sides. He was more than a little bit pissed at how the meeting had gone. Not only were they sending them into a massive incursion with little information, but they had also told him how to train Max. They were choosing to put the young priest in harm's way, and it wasn't acceptable.

When he reached the top of the steps, he paused to take a deep breath and relax his tense muscles. The last thing he needed was to send Max out there to start exorcising with the thought in his head that he wasn't ready for it. At the same time, Damian wouldn't let the Wise Men compromise Max's safety. He had been tasked to train the kid and keep him safe in the process. No matter what the repercussions were in the end, he would continue to do it his way.

He knew his place in the ranks and always tried to stay as respectful as possible. That said, he would not stand back and accept decisions that easily could—and most likely *would*—cost his trainee and friend his life. If Max were to die out there, it would fall on Damian's head and heart. He could not endure that. At the same time, though, they worked the same way any business did, and he took orders from the higher-ups in the church. There was a ranking system among them, but the Wise Men had to understand that Damian worked for an even higher power. He knew that God would not lead him down the wrong road, and he would make sure the church leadership didn't either.

The priest walked slowly toward the SUV. He would protect Max against all evil, even if it came in the form of those who should lead and protect them. One thing he'd learned from many years in the merc service was the fact that things weren't always what they seemed. Sometimes, evil disguised itself in familiar skin—or robes, in this case.

Damian opened the drivers-side door and climbed inside. He looked straight ahead and immediately put the car in drive, not saying a word to his passenger. They drove silently through the town, more slowly this time since there were now more people out and about, dawn having broken while he was in the meeting. The trainee glanced at him every few minutes, but he avoided eye contact and tried to calm his mind.

Max watched the early-morning activity and thoughts of easier times floated through his mind. By the time they reached the edge of town, though, he had tired of the silent treatment.

He looked at his mentor, chewing on his lip. "So, did they, like, fire you or something? If you're going rogue, we should talk, because I may want to get out."

Damian chuckled. "Wouldn't you like that? No, we have a mission. We leave for Scotland tomorrow."

"Scotland. Wow."

"Apparently, there is a cell kidnapping innocents, turning them, and sacrificing them to Moloch. On top of that, a portal was opened, and demons are mingled with the Damned, although they aren't hard to spot. We will meet mercs at the scene and exorcise as many Damned as we can. I'm not sure how many of each there are, but we will rely heavily on the mercs to eliminate the demons. Of course, I won't let us walk in without some sort of protection, but I gotta figure out how to get it there if we fly."

Max looked away for a moment. "So, this is a full-on incursion? Like, we roll up with mercs who take the demons down?"

Damian smiled. "That's right. This will be your first big incursion. Don't worry, I'll be with you the whole time. We'll do what we did before, only with a lot more help. Think about it—if we'd had mercs at the church, we would have been a lot safer. That is what we'll have in Scotland."

Max clutched his hands together in his lap. Damian noticed but didn't comment. "Well, I guess I had to pop that cherry at some point, right?" the young man said with false bravado. "But I'm glad I'll be there with you, learning what to do."

Damian didn't respond, and definitely wouldn't tell him that the orders were for him to go out on his own. He could tell from Max's reaction that he wasn't ready. The Wise Men had no idea how to train. They had some sort of agenda, but Damian didn't give a damn. He would keep his mentee safe, no matter what he had to do.

It was almost noon when they arrived at the house. Max helped unload the SUV and went quietly to his bedroom. Damian listened outside his door and heard him climb into bed. That was a good thing, since the exorcism exhausted him and the young priest needed to rest so he could be at full strength for the things ahead in the coming days. For once, Damian couldn't indulge his own weariness. So many things floated around in his head that he could barely keep one thought straight.

He changed into his pajamas and stared at his bed for several moments, anger tensing his muscles. Still pissed about his meeting, he knew if he laid down he would simply stare at the ceiling while the anger festered. He flipped the light off and walked to the small bar, where he selected a rocks glass. Tracing the different bottle tops with his finger, he selected a subtle and chill whiskey. Damian poured two fingers into his glass and swished it before taking a sip.

Ravi perked up as soon as the whiskey hit his tongue. *It's about fucking time. Seriously, I started to think that with all the stress we're under, our heads would explode. This was exactly what we needed. Hell, we needed it back in that room with the three Wise Douches.*

Damian laughed as he eased into his chair. *I can agree wholeheartedly with you on that one. It took everything I had to not flip out on them, although the last thing I want is to end up on some crazy security duty in the Amazon because I pissed them off.*

The demon grimaced. *Yeah, I don't like snakes or furry creatures or insects, so let's stay away from there.*

I thought you demons loved those things? Especially as a late-afternoon snack.

She made a gagging sound. *Some of us, believe it or not, actually have a modicum of class. I know, it's nuts, right?*

Damian shook his head as he stood and threw some logs in the fireplace. He squatted and started the blaze, using the poker to stoke it. His thoughts jumped from the upcoming trip to the mysteries that faced him, and he stared gloomily into the flames. There was so much going on, and he longed to relax. Thoughts of the cardinal constantly nagged in the back of his mind, however, and he had to scratch that itch. Seeing the three Wise Men earlier had ignited that inner burn again, and he couldn't help but recall the picture of them with the cardinal whenever he saw them. There had to be some connection.

When the fire blazed cheerfully, he opened the hidden safe to retrieve the top journal. He sat with his feet up, took a long sip of whiskey, and breathed deep, pulling the throw over his shoulders against the chill in the air.

Damian opened the journal to the second page. "Okay, Cardinal, let's figure out what secrets you're hiding."

October 31, 1965

After my last journal entry, things were quiet. The night air held a calm I had not known since I was a young boy playing in the courtyard of the monastery. The trees looked beautiful in their vibrant fall colors, the children laughed wildly, and the birds seemed to sing to me again. When I prayed, I felt my words were heard. When I lit the candles of worship, they glowed with a power I had not sensed before. The presence of God was all around me.

I went to bed last night tired from the day's work. The people of the parish had been blessed with plenty, but it took work to reap. It was good work, though, the kind that helped you remember exactly why you did what you did every day. I knew that All Hallows Eve lurked, but I suppose I hoped I could escape it without issues. After laying my head on the pillow, I stared at the clock. The time seemed to tick by faster than normal, and the clicks the hands made echoed like a drum through my chambers.

When it struck midnight, it was officially All Hallows Eve. I sat up in my bed, expectant, as if someone was destined to appear. After a few moments, I laughed, thinking that it was just my mind playing tricks on me. However, a few moments later, a loud thump sounded in my room, and wind whipped around wildly, blowing out the lamp. I clung to my sheets, uncertain what to do. He stood before me in the darkness, his eyes shining brightly through the shadows of night. His laughter bellowed, but only for a moment.

When I opened my eyes again, the lamp was lit and the demon was gone. I thought perhaps I had only dreamt it. I turned over, relieved, and fell asleep. This morning came too soon, with so much to do. I hurried from my chambers and did not return until nightfall. As I sat here in my pajamas, reading the word of the Lord, I glanced at a mark on the floor across the room. Curious, I walked to it and stopped, my breath catching in my throat. In the floor were deep gashes, as if something had clawed the wood.

My gaze shifted to the wall, where a message was written in dripping blood. It read, I will return at the stroke of midnight.

I watch the clock. It's 11:55.

CHAPTER ELEVEN

Max breathed heavily as he slowed the treadmill to a fast walk. He was warming up for a strong, healthy workout with Astaroth, and the upcoming fight constantly invaded his thoughts. It would be beyond his experience, and he was nervous. He knew he could exorcise and he knew that he could fight to a degree, but he had not tested those two things in such a large-scale situation before.

Astaroth was ready. *It's no use sitting there dwelling on it. Let's get some hand-to-hand combat in. Grab one of the dagger dummies and put it on the floor. You'll practice offense today.*

The young priest turned the treadmill off, grabbed his towel, and wiped his forehead before he retrieved one of the dummies. He twisted the pole to raise it to eye level and tossed his towel aside. *Okay. I'm ready.*

The demon thought carefully. *I'll call out moves for you to make. Try not to anticipate them. Just move with my words. Focus on the movements.*

Max nodded, rolled his shoulders, and stretched. He moved into position and waited. Astaroth began to bark simple but clear commands. Max gritted his teeth and attempted to complete each action. The dummy's head bounced a little, but mostly a tangle of arms whirled wildly around it. There was no grace to his movements. In fact, the harder he tried, the crazier it got.

Finally, after about five minutes of total chaos, Astaroth stopped him. *Stop. Stop. Good Lord, Maximus. You look like one of those waving tube men at the side of the road in a car dealership, only with six arms. You need to calm yourself and find your inner momentum. Focus your mind on each individual hand movement. Connect your mind with your hands so completely that you don't even remember my commands when you're finished. Keep this up, and that dummy will start fighting back. If that happens, we shut it down and find a new career— something safe like stuffing pillows or painting fences.*

Max dropped his arms to his side and shook his head. *We may need to eventually face the fact that putting me in combat could have unintended consequences. It could spark an international conflict.*

Astaroth chuckled. *No, no. Once you learn to focus on your movements, you'll see how easy it becomes. Come on, let's try again.*

The priest cracked his neck. *Ready when you are, Sensei.*

Max inhaled a deep, calming breath, closed his eyes, and tried to release the anxiety from his chest. He didn't want any distractions. Instinct told him that knowing how to defend and fight might be critical to his survival on the upcoming mission.

Astaroth started again. *Right punch to the neck, left punch to the chest. Right chop to the neck, left chop to the arm...*

The demon continued, paying close attention to every move the human made. Feeling the rhythm flow through him, Max opened his eyes and watched his movements. He knew his mind was responsible, but it felt almost as natural and thoughtless as walking down the street. His hands moved fluidly, with his elbows tucked in neatly. With every new round his motions became more fluid, and by the fifth round, his actions were twice as fast as when he had started.

Max smiled as he turned, trying new moves as they were called out to him. *Do you see this?*

Astaroth couldn't help but laugh. *I do. Concentrate. One more round and we break. When we come back, we will incorporate the legs.*

The trainee completed a final round of punches and swipes and finished with a loud battle cry. He stepped back from the dummy, pressed his palms together, and bowed. A round of applause sounded from the doorway with Damian's familiar chuckle a pleasant echo.

His mentor leaned against the wall, smiling widely. "You're getting better—much better. I'm happy about this. Maybe now you'll actually hit a demon when you swing at it."

Max faked a laugh as he took a swig of water. "Astaroth is trying to prepare me."

"Well, speaking of that, the Secretary called. We gotta get on the road. She pretty much threatened my life if we miss the flight."

Max laughed. "Well, I guess I better get on it then. I don't want to be killed by your weird robot stalker."

Damian nodded. "Exactly. I'll meet you downstairs."

Max gathered his things and headed to the guest bathroom. He hurried through a hot shower and dressed quickly, and it took only a few minutes to throw what he needed into his duffle bag and click the light off. In the garage, he was surprised to find that Damian had already packed the SUV with whatever they were taking. Max tossed his bag in the back and jumped inside.

He smirked. "You managed to pack the car on your own. Are you all right? Didn't stroke out?"

The older man chuckled. "Okay, wiseass. Sit back. Time to party."

Both men passed out within the first fifteen minutes of the flight. Damian had somehow managed to get them upgraded to first class, so Max had more than enough room to stretch out comfortably. He rested his head against the window and listened to the engines purring softly. His companion drooled on the edge of an inflatable neck pillow.

By the time they reached Scotland, both had gotten a short rest. They grabbed their carry-ons and headed to baggage claim. Damian pointed at the carousel. "Don't let any of our luggage get picked up inadvertently. There are very fragile things there. I got lucky with a special concession on this flight thanks to Katie, and they allowed me to check everything we need."

Max nodded, hurried to the luggage area, and retrieved the black duffels as they circled on the belt. Damian wandered toward the door, unsure of the next step. His phone buzzed with a message from the Secretary.

SUV out front. Address loaded in GPS. Don't forget the Wise Men's instructions.

The priest growled and shoved his phone into his pocket, slung his bag over his shoulder, and exited through the sliding doors. A blacked-out SUV waited at the curb. The driver's door opened, and a man in a dark suit and sunglasses emerged and handed the keys to Damian. Without a word, he turned and walked to a cab.

Max rushed out, pushing a loaded luggage cart. "Is that ours?"

Damian nodded. "Load everything in, my friend."

The trainee rolled his eyes and pushed the cart to the back. He lifted the bags quickly into the back and shut the door while Damian slid behind the wheel and glanced around for the GPS' on-switch. The system booted, and the address and directions popped up.

Max slid into the passenger seat and raised a brow. "They sure did think of everything."

Damian scoffed. "Yeah, except the details of what we'll walk into. We have nothing, so we should make an interesting entrance into a fight that the mercs started hours ago."

The younger man shrugged. "Maybe they will have finished the whole thing by the time we get there. We can sit around and enjoy Scotland for a hot minute before rushing back."

"Please, like the Wise Men would let that happen. You know they would sacrifice their own souls to see us do our jobs."

Max chuckled and relaxed as they drove to the incursion. It wasn't far, but rather than head for the city, they turned toward the country. When they arrived at the old farmhouse, they found the mercs already there. Demons raced everywhere, and gunfire plowed across the landscape. Things seemed completely out of hand as the beasts crawled up the house or were shot point blank in the fields.

Max exited the SUV with wide eyes and stared at the chaos in silence. Damian grabbed his arm, and the two loaded up with pistols, knives, their crosses, and their bibles. The older man caught and held his companion's attention. "I know it seems wild right now, but take a deep breath, okay? You'll get into the swing of it really fast, and I'll be right there with you."

The trainee nodded nervously. They crossed the field to where the mercs had gathered to reload and for water and medical attention. Damian elbowed Max lightly and nodded toward the group. "Let me do the talking, okay?"

One of the men inserted a new magazine in his pistol and looked up, recognizing Damian. He immediately jogged out to meet them. The priest put his hand out and shook the merc's hand. "I'm Damian, and this is Max. We're here for the exorcisms, and to help where we can."

The man nodded with a smile, squinting into the sunlight. "Yeah, man. I remember you. You were on Korbin's Killers for, like, *ever*."

Damian smiled. "That's right, I was. You look familiar too."

"I'm Charlie. I was on a New York team, and you and I fought a few battles together late in the merc season. It was when Katie was on your team but not yet the badass angel-demon she is now."

"Right. Yeah. Was that the fight where we took down that one-eyed bastard trying to pull a King Kong on the Statue of Liberty?"

Charlie howled and nodded. "Yes! That was one of them. You did the backflip off Lady Liberty's spikes and jammed your knife into that fucker's back. It was awesome. Good stuff."

Damian pointed to Max. "Max is my partner but is also in training. This will be his first all-out incursion. He should be with or near me the entire time."

Charlie shook the young man's hand. "Good to meet you, buddy. Just pay attention and watch for the fallers—the ones that jump from the ceiling. Other than that, do your thing and try to have fun. Worry and fear will only slow you down and make it more dangerous. If you need protection, the team has vests. Grab one. They'll recognize the priest getup."

"We're not here to fight so much as we were sent by the church to exorcise as many Damned as possible. Obviously not mercs, but any others we can save."

Charlie nodded. "Got it. Okay. Let me get on my comm."

He pressed the comm button on his ear and spoke quickly. "Team, we have two priests here, both Damned. One is ex-merc, the other a newbie. They're here to exorcise as many infected as they can. Help them out by either throwing them the infected or killing the demons to clear a path. We'll have to work together today. Kick ass, guys."

The team responded, ready and willing to help. It was a

relief to find someone who recognized him and didn't seem to have any problems with their role but also saw their firearms. Damian had always done things his way, which was why he had survived as long as he had.

Charlie pulled him aside and lowered his voice. "I'm all about saving the innocent if we can. I want you to know that. But understand that even though we'll do what we can to help you, this is a battle. Most likely we will have to kill a lot of the demons, even the infected ones, because you know how it is. When you're out there being attacked from all angles, you don't stop to think who could be exorcised. You fight for your life. Have some patience with the team, okay?"

The priest patted him on the shoulder. "I completely understand where you're coming from. We came with weapons, even though the church doesn't technically allow them. I know what these things are like, and sometimes it's your life or theirs. We'll eliminate as many of the pure demons as we can to help you guys out. We won't get in the way, and we won't put your team in any danger."

Charlie seemed relieved by that response. "You're welcome to any of our ammo or weapons. They're from your girl anyway. I'm gonna get out there and get my kills. I'm already past my personal quota, and I'm gonna see if I can double it."

Damian laughed and watched as the merc ran into the field, his guns already blasting. Max chuckled. "That guy is freaking wild. I love it."

The older man held both his cross and his weapon ready and smirked. "Mercs are a different breed. I know, because I'll always be one at heart."

CHAPTER TWELVE

"Where to first?" Max asked, his expression taut.

Damian glanced around, quickly assessing the scene. He nodded toward the farmhouse. "They have things under control out here. Let's go inside and see what damage we can do there."

Max pulled his knife, then shook his head and exchanged it for his gun. "I think I might need bigger this time around."

"Probably a good idea."

They moved across the field, alert for approaching demons. The older man glanced at his companion and sighed, then tossed his bible to him. Max juggled it for a moment before he gripped it firmly and stared at the name printed on the front cover. "What's this for? I have mine."

Damian kept his face expressionless, not liking the choice he had to make. "You'll have to help. There are too many for me to handle on my own. You've exorcised demons before, and this situation is no different."

Max wrinkled his nose uncertainly. "Except for the gazillion demons trying to take me down to hell with them."

He put his hand out to stop Max and faced him. "I've marked the prayers I like to use." He flipped through the bible, showing him the dog-eared pages. "The longer ones work better on larger infestations. Read them the way you would any other prayer."

Max holstered his gun and grabbed the satchel around his neck. He could feel the energy of the cross inside it. "What about you?"

Damian chuckled. "I know these prayers by heart. The bible is a prop for me. I'll be fine. The most important thing is to focus when you're saying them. Bring God into it like you do when you pray normally."

"Well, this should definitely be a learning experience for me, if nothing else."

"Remember one thing, though. If an infected can't be exorcised, you must take that person's life. They may look completely normal, and they may even prey on your sympathies, but hold strong. If the demon has completely taken over, there is nothing we can do for them. We have to neutralize the threat."

Max took a deep breath and straightened, mustering his inner strength. "I can do it."

Damian nodded. "Good. Now come on. Let's kick some ass."

They climbed the porch steps, and the older priest kicked the front door. It slammed open, grating on its hinges. Dust billowed, and light flooded the old stained floors. Damian slapped Max on the shoulder and smiled. "Good luck."

With that, he strode down the hall and kicked a demon square in the chest before blowing a hole in its forehead. He turned his head quickly when the walls creaked and rattled. A demon dropped from the ceiling and knocked him onto the floor, where they wrestled and the beast pinned Damian down. Its mouth opened wide, and its teeth dripped with saliva as it hissed in his face.

The priest struggled to bring his gun up between them. "Say hello to Moloch for me, asshole."

He pulled the trigger, and his adversary hurtled into the wall and slid to the floor. Damian stood, straightened his jacket, and fired another round into the demon's head. The beast squealed loudly and turned to dust. Damian moved into the kitchen and stopped when he saw a blonde woman at the stove, her back to him. He swallowed hard as she snarled and breathed heavily.

Damian held his cross up and cleared his throat, beginning the exorcism. As the woman turned, her eyes glowed bright red, and her teeth showed jagged and crimson. She held a frying pan containing a severed hand. As the words of the prayer increased in intensity, the Damned shook, dropped the pan, and slammed her hands over her ears. She growled loudly, stiffened, and fell.

The fiend rose from her body and screeched before bursting. Damian knelt beside the woman and found her pulse. It was weak, but he could tell she would pull through. As he stood, he glanced at the blood leaking onto the tiles from the frying pan. *"Bon appetit?"*

The priest raised his pistol instinctively as a loud crash

sounded right in front of him. A demon stood on the counter and knocked the dishes onto the floor. It swiped at Damian, but he evaded the deadly claws. "I don't think I invited you to dinner."

He squeezed the trigger twice, aiming for the skull. The beast fell backward and turned to ash before it hit the floor. Three more demons and one infected bolted through the doors, and Damian sighed, bracing himself on the edge of the counter. He aimed carefully and dispatched each of the demons with a single shot, but left the Damned untouched. Slowly, he walked forward, speaking the prayer.

The man cringed, and his hands turned to claws as his face twisted unnaturally. The priest spoke the prayer louder, but it had little effect. He shook his head, knowing the man was too far gone. "I'm sorry for this." He released the empty magazine from his gun and reloaded. "May God have mercy on your soul."

With that, he pulled the trigger, and the body hit the floor.

Max breathed heavily and held his pistol at the ready, taking one slow step at a time toward the upper floor. The claws of a demon scraped the walls above with a harsh sound that sent shivers down his spine, and he gripped his weapon tightly. Near the top, he paused to see if anything would jump out.

Astaroth sighed. *Go on, already. Sheesh.*

The young priest shook his head. *One thing I have*

learned is that anything is possible with these bastards. I know they get their rocks off by jumping out at me. Max listened for a moment, but he heard nothing. *They must have gone into one of the rooms.*

As he took another tentative step, a demon landed in front of him, hissing loudly. Max yelped and slammed his fist into its throat. The beast's eyes grew wide with surprise, and it grabbed its neck and stumbled back. Max squeezed his trigger three times, shattering the ugly face.

Astaroth chuckled. *Whoa, whoa, I think you got him. He won't smell anything for a long time.*

The creature turned to dust, and Max stomped up the rest of the steps. *I told you. They like to jump out unexpectedly.*

His demon scoffed. *You'll be fine, especially if you keep throat-punching the bitches like that.*

The trainee shook his head as he turned the corner and came face to face with a tall, redheaded woman with bright red eyes. He swallowed, lowered his gun, and held the bible open. The woman snarled, and her head jerked spasmodically as she walked toward him. He found one of the prayers and chanted as calmly as he could while she screamed loudly, the sound echoing down the hall.

Her claws morphed into human hands, and she grabbed her throat and thrashed violently. Her eyes went soft, and she looked at Max, one hand outstretched in a helpless gesture. "Please, stop. The demon is gone. Please, it hurts so much."

Max paused, but Astaroth gave him a jolt. *She's playing you. Keep going.*

He nodded and continued. The woman's face twisted with rage, and she shrieked and lunged at him. He side-stepped instinctively, and her body convulsed before it dropped to the floor. A demon floated free and hovered for a few moments as it writhed and screeched until finally, it erupted.

Max's shoulders relaxed, and he knelt beside the woman and made the sign of the cross. Her red eyes were blue pools of silent gratitude before she passed out. *She'll be all right.*

Astaroth sniffed the air. *She's the only one up here. Head back down to where the bulk of them are. You got this.*

Damian eliminated the demons in the kitchen and retreated down the hall, going past the staircase and into the living room. At least a dozen demons crawled in and out of windows and perched on furniture while some fought each other in the center of the room. The priest immediately opened fire, careful to avoid the infected among them. He stepped back and almost fell over another body. Looking over his shoulder, he saw that Max had joined the fray.

The older man reloaded and selected his next targets. "How you holding up?" he asked casually

Max fired a well-placed headshot. "Okay, I suppose. I exorcised one upstairs. You?"

Damian nodded. "Exorcised one, killed a bunch of demons."

For a long time, they simply focused on the seemingly endless stream of beasts with no time for exorcism. Max fired his last bullet and dropped the empty magazine on the floor. "I'm out."

His mentor tossed a new one to him. "My coat comes in handy sometimes."

Max grinned and shoved it home. "There are so many of them."

Droves of demons streamed toward them from the hallway. There were a few Damned mixed in, but there was no time to even think about exorcising them. A large demon burst through the front door, noticed Max and Damian, and growled loudly. The men looked at each other before they fired in unison at the beast's head.

The demon screamed and flailed its arms wildly, knocking Max back onto the steps. Before Damian could intervene, something slammed into his stomach. The force of the punch rolled him back into the wall, and he grunted at the impact and slid to the floor. Max narrowed his eyes as his mentor coughed, trying to catch his breath. He pushed up from the steps and shoved the creature aside to give the older man time. Under Astaroth's guidance, he kicked the demon hard in the side and followed up with a blow to its nose.

It shook its head and stumbled back, giving Damian time to find his feet. He leaped forward, wrapped his legs around the demon's neck, and flipped backward. The beast somersaulted onto the floor, and Damian shoved his gun into its head and fired. A soft whine cut off abruptly as it disintegrated.

The older man nodded his thanks as several Damned ran toward them, their skin hanging in peeling strips. Max sliced one through the neck with his dagger. He threw the second blade, and it thunked between the Damned's eyes. Both were so far gone that they turned to ash almost immediately.

They had given themselves a small breathing space, so Damian stepped beside Max and they looked out the door. He replaced his magazine and shook his head. "It looks like between us and the mercs, we've cleared out or exorcised at least half these bitches. This is the point where they usually try to make a break for it."

The trainee glanced to the right as demons crawled through the doorway and spread over the ceiling and walls like spiders. They perched there, hissing and staring at the two men.

"Uh, I think this might play out a little differently," Max remarked. "What do you think?"

Damian noted the shift in hostility. Normally, smaller ones would attack randomly but were mostly intent on finding food. These, however, were focused entirely on the two priests.

A demon dropped from the ceiling and stood, flexing its black-scaled shoulder muscles. The eyes were set wide apart, and its mouth drooped to reveal rows of hideous sharpened teeth. It scraped its claws on the floor and barked menacingly. Max's mouth dropped open. "Holy hell, what the fuck is it doing?"

Damian stared, having never seen that mentality in demons before. Without looking at his companion, he tapped Max's chest. "Language."

In the same breath, he lifted his gun and fired, striking the fiend in the chest. It looked at the hole and snarled as it lurched toward him. Damian held the weapon steady as he backed away, pulling the trigger again and again. Suddenly, Max launched himself onto the monster's shoulders, raised his dagger, and plunged it into the skull. The demon thrashed, and Max alighted to land beside his mentor.

Damian glanced at him with raised eyebrows. "Nice."

The younger man focused on the demon. "Thanks. I wasn't sure I would actually land on his shoulders. Just kind of winged it."

The beast howled loudly and fragmented, and the knife dropped. Max retrieved it and gestured out the door at a wall of demons creeping toward the mercs. "I didn't know they did this."

His mentor shook his head. "I've never seen it before, but it looks like an uprising. Things are completely out of hand. I don't know where they learned this, but it's not good news for us."

CHAPTER THIRTEEN

Damian grabbed Max's arm and pulled him toward the stairwell. Two shots each found a target among the demons creeping down the steps. The trainee glanced at the demons that were inching closer. "Where are we going?"

"I need a minute to think before they all start attacking."

Once upstairs, they moved cautiously down the hall, alert for other adversaries hiding there. It seemed they were all downstairs or outside, waiting to attack. Damian had never seen demons act like that in any previous incursion. It was obvious that to keep Max safe, he would have to go against the Wise Men's orders. There was no way he would send his trainee out there on his own and hope he stayed alive. The sheer distraction alone would probably get them both killed.

He stopped at the end of the hall in front of an open closet, glanced at the empty space, and thought for a moment. He wanted to clear his head but knew he didn't have much time.

Max looked bewildered. "Did I do something wrong?"

Damian's eyes softened, and he patted him on the chest. "No, you did a really good job. There was no way that either of us could exorcise. We were too inundated by demons to even think about it, and I'm now trying to think about our next plan of attack. Things are intense, and these demons are acting completely out of character."

Max straightened and puffed his chest out. "I'm ready. This is part of the job, and I want you to know that I can handle whatever comes my way. I got my hands of steel, my wits, and my weapons. If I have time to exorcise I will, but I won't hesitate to kill these guys. They obviously want to kill *us*, and they seem to have some sort of training."

Damian chuckled and nodded. "That they do, which is why it'll be incredibly difficult, especially for a newbie. These demons would give *Katie* a run for her money."

The trainee stomped his foot. "Then what are we waiting for? Let's take them down."

His mentor glanced at the closet and smirked. He shifted momentarily and thrust out his palm to strike Max in the chest. The young priest stumbled back, and Damian pushed him to the floor of the closet. Max shook his head, confused, and tried to stand.

Damian shoved the door almost shut and shook his head. "Sorry, kid. I promised I'd keep you alive. Try not to scream, or you'll call the demons right to this closet. When it's clear, I'll come get you out."

Max's eyes burned red as he tried again to stand, but the older man slammed the door and locked it from the outside. He stepped back as the trainee pounded the door and yelled, "Don't do this to me, Damian. This is my *job*! Dammit, let me out of this closet. So help me God, I'll knock the damn thing from its hinges."

A short silence was followed by a loud thud. Max groaned, and Damian chuckled and patted the door. "Just hold tight, buddy. This is not a fight for a newbie."

He rolled up his shirt sleeves. "All right, demons. You want to fuck around? I can play along with that."

Ravi hissed with laughter. *Oh. My. God. Seriously, how did you ever become a priest, much less stay a priest all these years? I don't know if they can fire priests, but if they can, how did you dodge that bullet? You are disobeying direct orders.*

Damian sneered. *Direct orders from a bunch of baboons who don't know their asses from their elbows. I'll be nice to their faces and I'll take the missions, but I'm tired of being pushed around. There is no way I'll get Max's ass torn up to prove something to them.*

She snickered. *The rebel priest, killing demons and throwing up gang signs. I'm sorry, but I've never seen a priest do something like that. Normally, they're very obedient and never question things.*

He headed purposefully down the hallway. *That's how people fucking get killed. They mess around, trying to play favorites and good boys, and someone does the wrong thing. I'll be damned if they test me on this. I've been a priest too long, and when God tells me something ain't right, I listen.*

Ravi exhaled a deep breath of relief. *I have to say, Damian, I'm proud of you. I know that might not mean much coming from a princess of darkness, but I am. Max is a kid, and while no one should have to deal with this, it's not worth risking his life. He definitely isn't ready to face the angry demon mob waiting for you downstairs.*

Damian paused at the stairs and glanced at the door. *To be honest with you, I don't know whether this is the right thing or not. I could have set myself and him up for failure, but the thought of fighting these assholes and worrying about him at the same time is more terrifying. That distraction will get me a talon in my chest.*

Or one in his, she added.

I couldn't bear the idea that I was the one to get him killed. If he dies, it'll be once he's fully prepared. He will be a master of his craft, and the decision to go down will be on him, not me.

Ravi was surprised and proud. *Well, just so you know, if you got killed protecting him, the kid would never survive it. He's tough, but not tough like that. I can tell. You made the right choice.*

Hearing a sudden sound from the room beside him, Damian kicked the door open and raised his gun. A young girl with glowing red eyes climbed the wall in the corner and hissed. He blinked several times, the tune from the amusement park haunting him. Thrusting the memory aside, he raised his hand and repeated the prayer. He lunged forward as the girl dropped from the wall, caught her, and laid her down on the floor as the demon rose and flashed out of existence. She was still alive.

Damian closed the door and shook his head to clear his mind. Ravi harrumphed as they reached the stairs. *You know what I think will be hilarious?*

He welcomed the distraction from his memories. *What?*

She laughed. *How absolutely livid he will be when he*

escapes that funky closet. I can already see him sitting in there fuming and plotting your demise.

Damian chuckled as he readied his weapons. *Better pissed than dead, in my opinion.*

Gunfire from one of the merc's automatic weapons sprayed the walls in the entrance to the house. Damian stood side by side with two fighters, and they systematically eliminated as many demons as they could. One snatched a Damned off the wall and slammed her to the floor. "Priest, I got one for you."

Damian raced over and whispered the exorcism while the merc held her down. She writhed and thrashed as the demon rose slowly from her body. As it erupted, Damian nodded to the woman fighter. "Thank you."

She dusted her hands off. "No problem. I find what you do admirable. I'm only sorry this is so chaotic that you can't help more of them."

Damian blasted a demon that lunged toward them. "Unfortunately, that is the name of the game in this business. I do what I can, and hope it is good enough for the church and for God."

The woman smiled and drew two short swords from her back. "That's all you can do."

She ran out the door, the other merc on her heels. Damian killed the last few demons inside and headed to the field out front to help where he could. Demons surged everywhere. They ran through the fields and pounced on mercs, mindlessly focused on the kill. Damian was standing on the porch trying to decide where he was needed when he heard Charlie call his name.

Across the field, the fighter held someone down in the long grasses. "Over here!"

He raced toward the merc and stopped when he saw the infected. Her skin was peeling, and her eyes were bright red. One glance was enough to know she couldn't be saved and he sighed and shook his head.

Charlie shot her once in the skull, killing her instantly. "Well, it was worth a shot. I haven't seen many infected that weren't completely taken over."

"It seems to be more like that every day, but I do what I can."

The fighter suddenly shoved Damian to the ground. The bewildered priest saw a demon leap forward and tackle Charlie, and they rolled in a tangle of limbs. The man winced as a claw raked his shoulder. Damian scrambled to his feet and ran to grab the fiend by the head and haul it off. He snatched the knife from his belt and thrust it hard, turning the aggressor to dust.

Panting, he turned to help Charlie to his feet. The fighter grimaced and rubbed his bleeding shoulder. "I'll be glad when this fucking day is over."

The field now seemed less overrun than before. "We're close. Come on, let's finish this shit on a high note."

They ran through the field as a unit, blasting demons right and left. Every so often they would find a Damned, but only one could be saved. Damian felt a rush of adrenaline, something he hadn't experienced since he'd left the Killers. While happy with his choice to rejoin the church, he couldn't deny it also felt good to be part of a team.

Kicking ass and taking names was his past, but at that moment, as he slammed demons to the ground in the Scottish countryside, he felt more alive than ever.

Astaroth chuckled. *Look at it this way. Instead of dying from a demon wound, you'll die from asbestos poisoning—a slow and painful goodbye.*

Max had pulled his knees to his chest, and his chin rested on top. *That's why I have you—to heal me of deadly diseases. I'll keep going until someone has to walk behind me and pick up my limbs.*

The demon scoffed. *Oh, no. If I'm stuck in here, I'll enjoy your death. We demons like pain and suffering.*

Thanks. Anyway, what does it matter? I'm stuck in a hall closet during a huge incursion.

Look, Damian took a big risk protecting you like this. I'm sure his bosses—those three lost Backstreet Boys—will not be happy about this. Take it as a lesson, and be happy that you don't have to lose an arm or something. Those demons were well-trained.

Max rolled his eyes. *That's exactly why I should be out there. If I can kick ass here, I can handle anything. I can get into the thick of it when we have a call.*

Astaroth didn't understand his irritation. *Like standing in the center of a cemetery as a ghost tries to smash you with a casket isn't "the thick of it?"*

That was nothing compared to demons. I just... Max paused and lifted his head to listen to a demon snarling outside. Three gunshots rang out, and everything went silent. He put his chin down and continued, *I hate being treated like a baby. I'll start cussing and drinking all the time. I'll figure out a way to say entire sentences using nothing but cuss words.*

Astaroth chuckled. *That sounds fun. You'll come off as a complete moron. Nice. I'm sure that's the way to get respect.*

Max groaned. *Doesn't matter. I'm stuck in here for eternity. Fuck a sack of cock and balls on a shitty-ass Tuesday morning. See, I can do it.*

Astaroth grimaced. *That sounds like a terrible time.*

Damian slammed a demon to the ground and sliced through its neck with his knife. The fiend turned to dust, and the priest straightened to look around. They had killed or exorcised every last threat there. He relaxed his shoulders, cleaned his knife, and sheathed it.

Charlie approached and clapped his approval. "That was some mighty fine slaying, Damian. You haven't lost your touch."

He laughed. "I wish that were true. You guys did a great job."

The fighter tilted his head with open curiosity. "Why are you doing this instead of raising hell with Katie in New York?"

"I have a new job. I do what I can to exorcise demons for the church."

Charlie shook his head and holstered his pistol. "Personally, I think it's a waste of your talent. To each his own, though. If you ever change your mind, give me a call. We can use all the good fighters we can get."

He handed Damian a card and turned to join his team, and the priest smiled. The battle had definitely been a blast, but it wasn't something he could do again. Things were different now. He crumpled the card and dropped it on the ground. As much as he was set in his current lifestyle, that card would be way too tempting.

CHAPTER FOURTEEN

Damian dragged his feet and rolled his arm to ease the shoulder joint. He opened the side door of the SUV and smiled as he put his gear away, thinking about old times in Vegas. There were good and bad memories for him. He zipped his duffel bag as the phone rang in his pocket. His first impulse was to ignore it and he hesitated for a moment, knowing it was the Secretary. After two more rings, he grumbled and rolled his eyes.

"Talk about a killjoy."

He pressed the Answer button, but before he could speak she yelled, "*Damian!* Damian, I don't know what to do with you anymore. We send you on a mission with explicit instructions, and you do whatever the hell you want. What *was* that today? Did you forget that you were no longer a mercenary? Did you forget the vows you took to the church? You aren't a merc anymore, and you need to remember that."

He groaned and turned to lean against the open door. She continued without giving him a chance to respond. "And what do you think the Wise Men will say about this? Do you think they'll stand back and allow you to break the rules over and over? I was shocked that they came to you with this after the hell you've wreaked with the other missions."

Damian sighed and shrugged. "They knew who I was when they asked me to join the team. I do things in the safest possible way and with the highest probability for survival. How do you think I've stayed alive all these years? It definitely wasn't luck, that's for damn sure. Look, you'd think that by now you would be used to the way I do things. Either way, the mission is complete. It's over and done with. Why does it matter how I get to that point? I saved everyone I could exorcise safely. Most of them were too far gone for me to even attempt it."

The Secretary scoffed. "I'm not sure how you know that, given the amount of ammo you unloaded on the demons."

He got defensive. "Look, warden, I won't be killed trying to exorcise when I know there's a minuscule chance it would work. It's about safety in these situations. They want me to live another day to continue the work, but at the same time, do stupid things that get people killed. No. I'll do it my way."

She sighed dramatically. "Damian, I understand that you know far better than me or even the Wise Men what it's like out there, but you have to follow the rules. They are there for a purpose, not simply to piss you off. As far as weapons go, I see why they are necessary. I do. That's half the reason the Wise Men haven't found out about the other times you've used them. This, though, will be virtually impossible to hide. They will want to see the footage, and you've put me in a very tough position."

Both lapsed into silence for a moment. Damian tried to calm himself, knowing that it was the Secretary's job to say those things. He opened his mouth to apologize for jumping down her throat, but she cut him off. "Damian?"

Damian smiled. "Yes, God?"

"I'm serious. Where the hell is Max?"

He jumped to his feet. "Holy shit. Uh, gotta go. Talk to you later."

The priest threw the phone onto the seat and raced toward the house. He waved at the mercs, who watched him with confused looks. Damian shook his head, breathing heavily as he jumped over an exorcised Damned in his path. *I can't fucking believe I forgot I locked Max in the closet.*

Ravi laughed hysterically, barely able to get her words out. *Oh...oh...this is fucking priceless. The priest was so worried about poor Max that he forgot him in the damn closet. Oh, boy. I can't... This is like the best thing that has ever happened.*

Damian snarled as he took the porch steps two at a time. *Seriously, I'm an asshole. Like, I won't be upset if Max punches me square in the nose. Okay, maybe I'll be upset, but it will be completely justified.*

The demon snorted in an effort to regain control. *That's the kind of shit that deserves a nut-punch. No kidding. Right in the nuts.*

He sneered as he started up the steps, slowing his speed.

You sound like Pandora. What is it with demons and nut-punches?

Ravi snickered. *We don't play by the rules.*

Damian reached the closet door and took a deep breath, straightened his jacket, and wiped the panic from his face. He clicked the lock and swung the door open with a smile. Max lifted his chin from his knees, his lips in a disapproving line. He raised an eyebrow but didn't say a word.

His mentor scratched his head and gestured over his shoulder. "Sorry, dude. I wanted to make sure there weren't any more demons lurking in the shadows. It wouldn't make much sense to pull you out only to get in a fight."

He grunted as he pulled Max to his feet and stepped back far enough that if the trainee swung, he could dodge it. Max dusted his pants off and stepped out, squinting at the light. He looked down the hall and then at the older man.

Damian chuckled nervously. "You do okay in there? It was a hell of a fight. Sorry it took so long to get you out. Better safe than sorry, though."

Max shoved his companion's chest hard. "It's actually funny."

"What is?"

"Oh, just that fifteen or twenty minutes ago, one of the mercs stood outside the closet talking to someone. Do you know what they said?"

Damian frowned. "No, what?"

Max looked down the hall and fixed his mentor with a hard look. "Just that they had gotten every last demon and you had been a real asset."

He stuttered the beginnings of a response, but Max rolled his eyes and held his hands up. "I can't believe you forgot me. You left me in a dank old closet where I'm sure at least a dozen mice had met their Maker. There were spiders in there that I don't think have ever been cataloged, not to mention that it smelled like a mixture of dog shit and one of Rose's lethal pies."

Damian sighed and shrugged. "I'm sorry. But hey, the Secretary had your back the whole time. In fact, she called to ask where you were."

Max glared at him. "Mmm. More like she called to reprimand you for not doing your job and then noticed that I was nowhere around."

He slapped the young man on the shoulder. "At least she noticed, right?"

Max sighed and shook his head. "I don't even know who the hell the Secretary is, but tell her thanks. Who knows how long it would have taken you to realize I wasn't around? I might have been in there for days."

Damian scoffed. "Nah, I would have noticed when it was time to load and you weren't there for the heavy lifting."

Max narrowed his eyes. "Great, I'm a fucking workhorse."

His mentor laughed loudly, gave him a thumbs-up, and swiped a cobweb from his shoulder. "Language!"

Max shook his head and hurried after him. "No. Uh-uh. No way. If you forget me in the closet of a rundown farm-house, I get to say a few bad words here and there. This is not something you can walk away from."

He stopped at the bottom of the stairs as Damian

walked outside whistling. Exasperated, he threw his arms in the air and groaned.

Damian looked at the ceiling when he heard a weight hit the floor. Ravi giggled. *What was that? Did he miss the dummy again with his hopeless kicks?*

The priest shook his head and sipped his whiskey. *Who knows? But I won't complain. He has put in double time, training with his demon. He needs it, too. I can only lock him in so many closets before the Wise Men catch on.*

She laughed. *Maybe next time you could lock him in a bathroom or something. At least then he can pace the floor angrily instead of sitting in the dark and dust.*

Better yet, I'll put a cage in the back of the SUV and trick him into it with books about tourism. When he goes inside, bang —the doors come down.

Ravi cleared her throat. *You* do *know your partner is a human, right? You can't lock him in a cage.*

Damian scoffed. *I do what I want. Besides, one day he will thank me for it. He will be alive and breathing.*

She snickered under her breath. *Yeah, like that will ever happen.*

The priest opened the cardinal's journal to the next entry. This was his downtime, and he was determined to put the clues together. He settled in near the fire and began to read.

November 15, 1965

Everything has gone downhill since All Hallows Eve. What I did that night for survival will haunt my mind for eternity. This is one of the few moments I feel safe writing this in my journal. The demon from that night seems to have gone back to where he came from. I suppose I did one of the many favors that I owe. Nonetheless, I hope not to run into his kind again.

His bright red eyes and snarling jaws will give me nightmares for eternity. The demon he was looking for could not be found, but no matter. He took someone else. I received my first medallion, a trade for a tiny piece of my soul when the time comes. I will guard it with my life.

The church has no suspicion of my involvement in anything, and I must keep it that way. One whisper and I will have failed them and the demon. I'm not really sure which will be worse. The bells are ringing for supper at the chapel, and hopefully, sleep will finally find me tonight. God knows, I never know when the next task will come.

Until next time.

Damian closed the journal and rested his chin in his hand. This entry was shorter, and it left more questions than answers. He began to see that this mystery would take a very long time to solve, but he vowed to push forward. The most powerful religious organization in the world was involved, and he wanted to get to the bottom of it.

Ravi was silent for a moment and then spoke carefully. *Look, I know you're the priest of all trades. I know that Sherlock Holmes secretly lives inside you, but I think you're being reckless. I personally believe you should leave this whole thing alone.*

Damian tilted his head thoughtfully. *I don't understand. I thought you believed, as I do, that this is important. Besides, I cannot walk away now.*

She exhaled sharply. *Remember what that ghost said? "He*

shall find you, and when he does, all of the fallen will gather at your doorstep." Then boom, he exploded.

He set the book on the table. *Yes, I remember. Do you know what that might mean?*

Her cough was obviously fake. *Uh, no, I have no idea. But it sounded ominous, and I think you should put more stock in it than you do. This isn't a game, Damian. You can't ignore things because you want to.*

Damian raised an eyebrow, sure she knew more. *You know what, Ravi? One of these days, you'll realize that I'm not only your vessel, but I'm also your only ally. You will stop hiding behind your secrets. I will not judge you because you have a past, but I will blame you if those secrets get in the way of solving this or any other mystery that could save lives. There is no sense in hiding from the truth.*

Ravi said nothing for several moments. *Yeah? Yeah? Well, whatever. One day, you'll wear orthopedic shoes, shit your diaper, and say hello to the invalid next door. Fortunately for you, as it is for me, today isn't that day.*

He stood and returned the journal to the safe. *One day you'll hold back too much, and it will cost us both our lives and our freedom. But do as you will. You* are *a demon, after all. It doesn't surprise me that you are stubborn. What surprises me is that whatever you're holding back scares you. I didn't think you scared easily.*

The demon fumed. *Go fuck yourself, priest. Not everything is as cut and dried as you would like it to be. Even your precious Katie has secrets she will never reveal to you.*

Damian closed the safe. *You're right. The difference is, if she had a secret that would move us forward in this war, she would bite the bullet and tell us.*

Ravi sulked in the shadows of her prison and remained obdurately silent. Part of him felt bad for barking at her like that, but it was time she knew how he felt. Whether it did any good, only time would tell. For now, he would focus on work and the cardinal, and his demon could take her time.

CHAPTER FIFTEEN

"Ahhh." Damian sighed, put his feet up, and sipped his hot coffee.

The sun was out, but fall had arrived. The leaves were colorful, the breeze was cold, and they'd had their first frost of the year. It would be his first full autumn and winter in London, and he hoped it wouldn't be worse than those he had experienced in the States. He shivered slightly, pulled his collar up, and tucked the scarf more securely around his neck. He wore black fingerless gloves, a pair he'd owned since he'd joined the mercs. They were rather the worse for wear at that point, but they did the job.

Ravi snickered. *You look like an old hobo in those things. And what is the point? You want to keep your palms warm, but fuck your digits? They can freeze?*

Damian chuckled as he opened his fallen angel book and flipped to his place. Notes were written on the sides, obviously in Pandora's hand. He took his time reading the page from top to bottom before he tried to make sense of the annotations. It seemed that was her way to ease her frustration, but they were hilarious. On the top of the page, written in large letters, was Pandora's sassy attitude.

If you are reading this book, save yourself time and burn the fucking thing.

He smirked and turned the book sideways to read the next scribble.

Apparently this writer has no idea what an angel is, much less a fallen one. Are all humans this fucking dumb? Angels of any kind don't have magical powers, you fucking idiot. Move out of your mom's basement.

Damian laughed loudly, covering his mouth. Along the binding of the book was another message to the reader.

Eat a dick, bozo. If you think fallen angels are all death and destruction, you have another think coming. Maybe you deserve a little death and destruction...of your asshole.

He shook his head and sipped his coffee. She had underlined and crossed out information throughout the text. He didn't know when Pandora had worked on it, but she must have been more than bored. It made him think about Katie and Pandora, and he felt homesick for a moment.

Ravi chuckled. *This is what it takes for you to feel homesick? Vulgar language by the Queen of hell talking about the destruction of someone's asshole?*

Damian shrugged. *Hey, I didn't pick my friends. They picked me. I guess they grew on me more than I thought they would. Even Pandora, who turned out to be a surprising ally.*

He turned the page and paused as the sounds of scraping footsteps came from Rose's doorway. She stepped slowly out of the shadows, her gaze fixed on the broken paving. Damian straightened quietly, shut the book, and put it on the table. She hadn't noticed him, and he wanted it to stay that way. He wanted to see what she was doing.

Her dress was dirty and wrinkled, and her hair was no longer pulled back in a perfect bun. The silver strands stuck in all directions and framed her wrinkled face. She seemed to have aged ten years overnight. Her back hunched as she walked, and her left foot dragged slightly. The bones in her curled hands looked twisted and frail, and her eyes were a constant deep red that shimmered in the shadows around her.

"Damn broom," she mumbled, followed by inaudible sounds.

Her voice was deep and scratchy, unlike the Rose he knew. It was obvious that at that moment, the demon had taken her over. Every once in a while, her voice would emerge between the words of the snarling, snapping creature. Damian could hear a plea in her tone, and it broke his heart. The beast would take control quickly, and her head would twitch to the side.

Damian pulled one leg over the other and watched as she attempted to use the broom. She was clumsy and had difficulty moving it and her body at the same time. The demon tried to use her like a puppet, but it was clear he hadn't mastered human movement yet.

Ravi groaned. *Looks like you might be losing old Grammy over there. I can barely sense her human presence.*

Damian sneered. *This is bullshit. She is a fighter, but she shouldn't have to be. She doesn't deserve this.*

Damian, none of them do. You got lucky, like the other mercs. So many humans are taken, and no one even notices.

He balled his fist. *Does that make it right? I'll answer that for you. No, it fucking doesn't.*

Rose dropped the broom, and a deep demonic voice snapped, "Pick it up! Useless sack of meat. Either die and let me go or let me have what's left of this crippled old body."

An echo of her voice shimmered across the courtyard like a ghost in the wind. It sent chills up Damian's spine as he sat there and watched her struggle. Her eyes flashed a brighter red as she retrieved the broom and continued to sweep. The demon, lost in trying to take her over, hadn't noticed him. Damian held his coffee tightly for a second before he slammed the cup on the table.

Rose turned and looked at him. He narrowed his eyes, dropped his feet from the chair, and leaned forward on his elbows. Her eyes flashed again, and the demon grumbled. She turned and ran back into the house, slamming the door behind her. Damian straightened and shook his head. *I don't understand how the church—or* why *the church—would do this to her. If she was so devout, why wouldn't they want to ease her suffering?*

Ravi exhaled slowly. *I don't know, Damian. Maybe it was her choice. Maybe she wanted to fight the demon on her own, but the church seems to have more secrets than Lucifer these days.*

Damian scoffed. *You're telling me. I can't get a straight answer out of anyone. Still, there must be a limit. They must eventually allow me to do something for her, right?*

I wouldn't bet on it, especially after the whole debacle in Scotland. You'll be lucky to get permission to take a piss at this point.

He tapped his fingers on the table and glanced at his phone. The more he thought about it, the more frustration built in the pit of his chest. Ravi could tell he was worked up. *Calm down, Damian. If you're going to do what I think you are, you might want to think twice.*

I don't need to think twice about what is right. When something is wrong, you need to say it's wrong, no matter who will come down on you.

Damian scrolled through the phone and found the Secretary's number. He hovered his finger over the call button, but before he could press it, the device rang in his hand. He squinted at the screen. Leaning his head back, he dropped his hand to his lap and groaned loudly, rolling his eyes. "You have got to be shitting me right now."

He took a deep breath and clicked the Answer button. "Please tell me this is some strange coincidence and that you're not calling me because I was about to call you. I may work for you and the Wise Men, but I do have a right to my privacy, for fuck's sake."

The Secretary cleared her throat. "That's some language for a priest, although I am not in the least surprised. Your file is a mile thick, and it took me three months of research before I understood who I would be directing. And what exactly would you consider a coincidence?"

Damian scowled. "Not you watching me and knowing I was about to call you. You calling to say hi and to apologize for being a crazy stalker, maybe. Perhaps asking me how to upload information to your mainframe. You know, the non-creepy shit."

She stopped typing and chuckled. "What can I do for you today, Damian? Are you calling to find out what the rules of your job are? Because you don't seem to be able to follow them. You went through the basic courses, and I know you are an intelligent man. This can't be that difficult."

He smirked. "My, aren't you in a snippy mood today? No, I'm not calling for a refresher on rules. Quite the opposite."

The Secretary spoke slowly and carefully. "How so?"

Damian tapped his finger on the edge of his mug. "I was actually calling about breaking another of them."

She exhaled a long, deep breath and adjusted the phone. "Okay, I think I'm ready for it. What rule are you breaking today?"

He glanced at Rose's door. "My neighbor, the elderly infected lady."

"Mmm, Rose. Yes, I know who she is."

Damian nodded. "Well, she looks terrible. She is morphing into a full demon. Even her voice isn't her own. My demon can't smell her human soul at all. That creature is taking control of her, and she is tortured almost every second of the day. It's ridiculous on so many levels. I haven't seen an infected like this before. Usually, when they're in this bad shape, they're attacking. Her body is too old for that, and I heard the demon trying to coax her into death. She isn't giving in, though, and I can only imagine how hard that is on her."

He waited for her to say something, but when she didn't, he continued, "I wanted to ask if I could take steps to help her. It doesn't even need to be a full exorcism, merely something to lift some of the weight off her shoulders. She is a devout Christian, and shouldn't have to suffer through this alone until death."

The Secretary began typing again. "The answer is no. Look, Damian, I appreciate the concern and empathy you have for this woman. That's one of the reasons you're so well respected in this church. At the same time, it has been made very clear to you that no one is to intervene in Rose's life or her struggles with said demon. You have your orders when it comes to her."

Damian growled. "This is bullshit, Secretary, and you know it. You won't even give me a good reason."

The short silence seemed interminable. "The truth is, I don't need to give you a reason. You need to trust the church. Even if I wanted to give you a reason, I couldn't. They don't explain every choice they make."

The priest held the phone angrily in front of him. "Then maybe you should start doing a bit of damn research for yourself. Stop hiding behind your telephone!"

He pressed the End button and hung up, slammed the phone on the table, and shook his head. At that point he was livid, unable to fully comprehend that he had just hung up on his only ally in the circle of leaders of the church. He didn't care, though. The decision was stupid and left his neighbor struggling and suffering.

As he sat there fuming, the front door opened and Max appeared, squinting against the light. Damian raised an eyebrow, his angry lips now twitching into a smile. The trainee wore a pair of black fleece pajama pants with bright orange jack-o-lanterns printed between little cursive Happy Halloweens. His bright orange tee featured a carved pumpkin.

Max caught his mentor's startled expression and glanced briefly at his shirt before he shrugged and sat. "What?" He smirked. "I like Halloween, and my mom bought me these. She always gets interesting pajamas since she can't buy me any other clothes."

The older priest laughed at a mental picture of Max growing up over the years with a fresh pair of jammies for every holiday. The kid was proud of them too, which made it even funnier. The lighthearted moment eased a little of Damian's anger, and he leaned back and lifted his cup in a mock toast.

"Max, this is why we make a really fucking good team. I handle the shit part of the job—the demons, the politics, and the secrets. You handle my horrible moods with God-awful pajamas and stories of your twelve-year-old attitude toward your mom. Well done, kid. Well done."

Max frowned, looking a little uncertain. He crossed one leg over the other, highlighting a pair of puffy pumpkin slippers and bat-printed socks. "Glad I can be of service. Wait until you see the ones she sends me for Christmas. I couldn't roll over in last year's—the stuffed antlers on the shirt made it feel like I was sleeping on a moose."

Tears welled in Damian's eyes with renewed laughter. "Thank God you don't observe Static Electricity Day. You might kill us all."

"Is there really a Static Electricity Day?"

"Sure the hell is," Damian affirmed, laughter still bubbling. "It's January ninth, but please try to refrain. We don't need the house going up in smoke."

CHAPTER SIXTEEN

Max swallowed the last of his coffee and stood. "Well, I'd better get dressed. It's tempting to sit around in my pajamas, but that would be frowned on, I suppose."

His mentor stretched lazily. "Yeah, I should change out of my cleaning clothes and get decent for the day."

They headed indoors, and Max rinsed the cups as Damian headed to his room. He opened the closet and hesitated for only a moment before selecting his new suit. Ravi cheered. *Finally! I wondered if you would ever wear the thing. I mean, I know it cost a pretty penny, but you'll never appreciate it if it's hidden in the closet.*

Damian chuckled. *I feel like it's a brand-new wand or something.*

She sniffed. *Might as well be. I mean, it's beautiful.*

He dressed, grabbed his hat and the long umbrella, and headed to the living room. Max hadn't appeared, so Damian wandered the room. He ran his finger over the layer of dust that had collected on the shelves and scowled. Thankfully, Max opened his door and distracted him from any thought of cleaning.

"Grab your coat," he told the trainee. "It's the perfect day for a walk to clear our minds."

Max raised a brow and smirked. "When did you become a cover for GQ? That suit looks like it cost more than my soul."

Damian laughed and shook the umbrella at him. "It probably did."

Max shrugged into his jacket. Tentatively, he ran his finger over Damian's sleeve. "Maybe I should think about wearing a nice suit every once in a while."

"I think you should. Although to afford it after the cut the church takes you'll have to kill about six demons, and that's once you're out of training."

The young man snorted disdainfully. "I can do that in about an hour with the incursions you take me on."

Max closed the door behind them and glanced at the broom, which still lay on the ground. Familiar fury rushed through Damian along with concern. Rose had not come back outside.

"I haven't seen Rose lately," Max observed thoughtfully as they traversed the courtyard. "No pies, no smiles, no sweeping. It's been oddly and scarily quiet out here, and I have to admit I don't like it."

Damian held the gate open for him. "I know. Trust me, I noticed. I'm working on a plan. For now, though, we do what we do."

The young man shoved his hands in his pockets and looked happily at the blue sky. "Can I ask you something?"

"Sure. What's up? Babies come from the stork."

Max chuckled. "Yeah, so I've heard. No, I wondered why you were so angry when you left the meeting with the Wise Men the other night. You tried to play it off like nothing was wrong, but you have to realize I have spent enough time with you to know it was bullshit. I could also tell you weren't in the mood to talk about it."

Damian cleared his throat and swung his folded umbrella at his side. "Max, doing what is right and following the orders of the church are sometimes two completely different things. There are times when they tell you one thing while your gut or your prayers tell you another. Those lines are often blurred, although at other times the lines are more than obvious. You have to decide which repercussions you are comfortable with—the reprimand of the church or that of your own conscience. It's often a hard decision."

The trainee nodded, recognizing that no further explanation would be forthcoming. "Is that what's hard about Rose?"

"Yeah. The lines in her case are obviously in conflict. To me, there is no question. The woman is infected, her demon has almost taken her over completely, and she needs either release or help. Then I remember who I work for, and how I took a vow to trust and protect the church. That sometimes means following orders that you don't understand or agree with. Sometimes, it will enrage you, and sometimes it will make you incredibly sad. It's a hard thing."

Max pointed at a coffee stand on the corner. "You want a cup?"

"Sure."

The young priest paid the vendor and handed his mentor a cup. Damian wrapped his hands around it and heat surged through his palms. Holding a hot drink was one thing he loved when he was cold. It seemed to soothe his entire soul, and after the battle the day before, he needed something warm and uncomplicated.

They walked on between the people going about their day. Max chuckled at a shop owner hanging a picture of Katie in the store window. "She seems to be all the rage."

Damian noticed the picture and laughed. "Wow, I suppose so. You know what, though? I'm not upset in the least. She doesn't always follow the rules, sure, but she gets stuff done, and she saves lives. That motivates me."

They left the main part of town and started down a long suburban street. Max smiled to himself as a memory surfaced. "I want to tell you a story from my childhood."

"All right. I like that. Whatcha got?"

Max laughed. "It's a moral-of-the-story kind of thing. When I was about thirteen, I hit that stage where I wanted things. Normal kids wanted CD players and game systems —that kind of thing. Me? I wanted to tithe on my own. I wanted to go on mission trips. My parents weren't poor, but my father was a hard-working man. He wanted me to understand the value of money and why it meant so much to give to the church, so I found a job."

"You sound like you have good parents."

"I didn't always see it, but yes, they are. Anyway, I delivered groceries for the local deli for extra money. My town was small, and I could put them on my bike or the trailer I rigged up and go anywhere in our area. I was paid every day for the work I did, and I worked whenever I wasn't in school or studying."

Damian smiled, imagining a young, enthusiastic priest-in-the-making. "Sounds like you learned from your father."

"I did. Then I had all this money, and I didn't know what to do with it. I wasn't interested in cool stuff, so I walked into the deacon's office one day and donated the whole lot to the church. I never thought to keep five bucks in my pocket for emergencies. I figured the church had bigger problems and needed the money more than me."

They turned a corner and kept walking. Max was thoughtful for a moment before continuing, "One day, I checked on one of the older people in the neighborhood, Mrs. Shale. She lived in the smallest house in town and didn't have a car, and most of the time her food was donated by the church. I found her laid up in bed, but she had no money for medication. It was relatively simple, over-the-counter kind of stuff. I didn't know it would keep her from getting pneumonia, though."

Damian sighed. "That's a shame. What did you do?"

Max drew a long breath and shrugged. "I didn't have the money either and asked one of the priests. He told me God would take care of her. It was incredibly frustrating. In the end, I stole the medication, and the church found out. They were harder to explain to than my parents were. I felt it was the right thing to do, even though it broke all the rules I'd been taught. It seemed wrong that people had to beg to save their lives."

The older man paused and looked at his companion. He patted him on the shoulder and laughed. "I think you were born for this job, Max. Not many people think that way anymore. We leave our elderly to fend for themselves while the world goes on. What happened to Mrs. Shale?"

Max frowned. "She died two months later from pneumonia when she ran out of medicine and had no one to ask. But at least for a few months, she felt better and could spend time gardening or sitting on her porch. I checked on her now and then from afar."

Damian shook his head, astounded. "You surprise me every day, young Padawan, although your fighting skills reflect your background."

Max smirked, knowing his mentor was teasing. "That will get better—or not—but either way, I'll be dangerous."

"The question is, to whom?"

They laughed and continued their walk. Damian turned his collar up and used his umbrella as a cane. "This has always been my favorite time of year. The leaves change colors, and it starts to get spooky."

"Right, like we need more spookiness in our lives. We hunt demons and have a pie-wielding old lady across the courtyard."

Damian sighed. "I have a feeling she won't be with us much longer, at least not in Rose form. The demon has almost taken full control, and I am not allowed to help her."

Max shoved his hands in his pockets in irritation. "That sucks. She doesn't deserve that life or death. I don't understand the church sometimes, but I have to say, she may be better off if the demon takes over. It has to be exhausting to fight him off with her limited ability."

"It's a shame. A damn shame. Who will sweep the patio?"

"And who will make me disgusting poisoned pies?" Max grinned. "And no whisper of a thrill, dodging planters when I go home. Though if the demon stays, he may continue."

Damian glanced at him. "I wouldn't count on it. He seems to struggle with motor skills, and can't even hold the broom. He would probably burn the place down while baking."

Max rolled his eyes as they reached the end of a cul-de-sac. "That would be just what we need."

The older man put his hand on his companion's shoulder. "Do you hear that?"

Shrieking and screaming echoed from the house on the corner. They turned toward an old Victorian-style home with large front pillars, a well-manicured lawn, and a wreath on the door. At first, it seemed incongruous for those sounds to come from there. It was nothing like the haunted rundown houses they usually found themselves in, but the shrieking grew louder as they moved closer.

Max looked at the upstairs windows. At first, he could see directly into the expensively-decorated space, but the apertures suddenly darkened. A loud menacing laugh sounded, and he stumbled off the curb. Damian pointed at the window where thick red liquid seeped down the panes, covering them.

The trainee was in shock. "Did we just happen to walk up on a haunted house, or did you plan this?"

Damian was just as surprised. "I didn't plan it, although I am glad we are here for it."

Max's jaw dropped. "*Glad*? I'm not sure that's the word I'd use. Glad is more like, you made it to dinner before all the turkey was scavenged. This is more like, can I rewind and ignore?"

Damian took one last sip of his coffee, emptied the rest on the road, and tossed the cup into a handy trashcan. "Max, I think it's time we did a little something on our own and saved souls without being told to. Trust me, it's a real morale-booster."

The trainee wasn't convinced. "Oh, sure, until you lose an eye or an arm."

The older priest simply patted him on the shoulder and set off toward the house. Max groaned and ditched his cup. "Wasting a perfectly good cup of coffee. It's a travesty."

Astaroth yawned. *Walking into a haunted house without a perfectly good cup of coffee is the real travesty, but I understand. You aren't talented enough to have one hand occupied.*

Max rolled his eyes, ignoring the comment as he jogged to where Damian stood in the front yard, studying the house. "You really have to give me a heads-up on these things."

Damian's grin danced with mischief. "Hey, Max?"

"Mmm?"

"We're doing an exorcism. Is that enough notice?"

CHAPTER SEVENTEEN

Max leaned closer to the front door, his ear almost touching it. For several moments, all was silent. As he touched the wood, a loud bang rattled the door in its frame. The young priest recoiled. Damian glanced at him and chuckled. "I assume you've reached a conclusion?"

He nodded at his mentor, his expression solemn. "This house is haunted."

Damian laughed and shook his head. "My, my, aren't you a regular Sherlock Holmes? We might as well head right in there. No use standing on the porch."

Max gulped and patted the front of his shirt. His eyes went wide, and he felt inside his jacket to find nothing but the coffee receipt. "Well, damn. I left my cross and bible back at the house. I never thought a leisurely walk in London would bring me face to face with an angry ghost."

"I've learned to always be ready for a fight. Demons appear at the most inopportune times. They have no idea what it takes to go in there and do battle."

"Or they do and are smarter than us." Max shook his head. "Surprise is a really good tactic."

Damian drew his bible and gloves casually from his pockets. "Well, it worked. I'm very surprised. Now, let's not dally. I would love another cup of warm coffee to stave this chill breeze off."

He handed the items to Max, who took them suspiciously and glared at the old leather gloves etched with burn marks. Damian rolled his hands expressively. "Put them on. We don't have time for your melodramatic thought process. We have a house to clear."

The young priest donned the gloves and flexed his hands while Damian used a handkerchief to retrieve his cross and placed it on top of the bible. Max looked at it with surprise, then picked it up. "What is this? Are you giving up already? I didn't come here to watch you commit suicide in a haunted house. How would I explain that to anyone? They'd think I murdered you."

Damian chuckled. "I know. It would be my parting gift to you—a little snark to go along with the life of demon hunting. You'd appreciate it later. But alas, no, I am not here to kill myself. These things are on loan for this fight. I'm handing you the reins for this exorcism. I want you to take the lead."

Max shook his head and took a hasty step back. "That's not possible. I mean, two days ago I was locked in a closet, and now you want me to be in charge?"

"You're ready. You've watched me several times, and this isn't an incursion, merely a simple exorcism. You can do this, Max. And don't worry. I'll be right beside you—or behind you—just in case."

"Just in case the demon cuts me to bits," he retorted

His mentor chuckled. "No, just in case you need support, but you'll be fine. I wouldn't have you do it if I didn't think you were ready. But please don't try your karate moves unless it's absolutely necessary."

Max rolled his eyes and swallowed hard as the door rattled once more. He tapped the doorknob tentatively, making sure it wasn't hot. Damian nodded approvingly. "Very good. You *are* learning."

It was cool to the touch, so he turned the knob and pushed the door open. A few inches in, it was jerked from his hands and slammed against the wall. Max glanced at Damian but stepped forward, and they moved warily and remained alert. When they cleared the entrance, the door slammed shut behind them and the lights flickered in the large chandelier that swayed above their heads.

Damian noted that Max didn't flinch when the door slammed. As the young priest grew into his responsibilities, his fear began to slowly melt, exactly as it should.

Max studied the large entryway with tall ceilings, shining hardwood floors, and beautiful paintings. A small table in the center held a vase. Directly ahead was a tall winding staircase, and to their right, a hall lined with doors. The house had obviously been remodeled recently.

The older man cleared his throat. "I've seen homes like this before. They started out as ramblers, the kitchen to your left, and living room ahead. The second floor was added more recently. I would say you should stick to the ground floor."

Max held the cross tightly in his hand. "But how do I

find the heart if I know nothing about the haunting or the house?"

Damian shifted his stance and glanced toward the hall. "The heart must be located. We usually know it beforehand because someone else has found it. *You* have to find it now."

The trainee walked to the stairs and looked up. Despite the manifestation on the windows seen outside, the upper level was dark and quiet. He paused in the entrance to the living room, where nothing was disturbed and a grand piano stood by the bay windows. Shaking his head, he crept forward to listen at the swinging door to the kitchen. The house had gone completely silent since they had arrived. Tapping his fingers on the bible, he moved to the center of the living room again and closed his eyes, concentrating hard.

Damian kept watch, making sure nothing snuck up on them. Ravi yawned loudly. *This is interesting. Junior looks unsure. Why don't you push him?*

He shook his head. *This is his exorcism. I won't always be here. Do you sense any demons in the house?*

Ravi sniffed. *Nah. There isn't anything within ten miles of here except me—and that stuck-up asshole inside Max, of course.*

You're getting pretty good at this, my little hound dog. He smirked in amusement.

The demon gasped. *I will give you the worst case of diarrhea ever. Don't you dare disrespect my magnificence in that manner. Man, it's good you're a priest. The ladies would hate you.*

Damian snickered. *That is probably true, although I do have a suave side in there somewhere. I have kept it locked in a box for so long that it may be a tad rusty, though.*

Oh, yeah, okay, Grandpa. Keep that shit locked up. No one wants to see that.

Max sighed, grabbing his mentor's attention. He looked completely unsure of himself, and Damian squeezed his arm. "This is the moment when you have to rely on your skills. Go with your instinct here. You can ask your demon, but they generally lack knowledge when it comes to ghosts. If your instincts fail, go with logic. There aren't many places in here the spirit could use as the heart. What does your gut tell you?"

The trainee centered himself, closed his eyes, and drew a deep breath. Tingles shot through his body, and images of the different rooms flipped through his mind like a deck of cards. When they slowed, he realized he knew exactly where the heart was, as if it had called to him. He opened his eyes and pointed at the door leading to the kitchen. "It's there, in the kitchen."

Damian patted him on the back. "Good. Now, remember to assess the situation before rushing into the room. Never stick your head in first unless you absolutely have to. Your safety is imperative."

Max gripped the bible and nodded as he walked quietly to the door. He breathed deeply and pushed it open barely enough to see inside. "I was right."

His companion peeked around him. A ghostly figure stood between the island and the stove. It seemed to be chopping vegetables and cooking something. There was no food, but he used the cookware like there was. The apparition was draped in a chef's coat and wore a tall chef's hat. Half his face was burnt to a crisp. The priests backed back out before the entity noticed them.

"Do you think he was killed here?" Max asked.

Damian shrugged. "It's hard to say. From the looks of him, he isn't from when the house was first built. It's possible the person or persons who live here had something to do with his death. It's also possible this is his home. There have been cases where someone dies at an office, restaurant, or somewhere else and comes home to settle in. They haunt their own house and don't understand why their loved ones fear them. This often creates rage, and that's when things can get ugly. This fellow seems content to cut his imaginary carrots and cook with nothing in the pan. Hopefully, that means that you can expel him quickly."

Max nodded. "Then maybe he won't be as bad as the others."

The older man shook his head in warning. "Don't underestimate him. We are intruders prepared to send him from this world, something he doesn't fully understand right now. It is the equivalent of someone breaking into our home and trying to kill us. He will fight back, but maybe we can do this quickly and painlessly."

Max opened the bible to a prayer, read it through quickly, and gripped the cross. "All right, here goes nothing. Hopefully, this guy wants to make crepes in heaven because he can't stay here."

Damian laughed and followed as the young priest pushed the door open and walked cautiously inside. Hopefully, the ghost wouldn't notice them for a while. Max stepped to the side, and his mentor let the door swing shut behind them. They pressed against the wall for a moment, watching as the apparition whistled happily, sprinkled non-existent spices into the empty pan, and shook it a little before placing it on the medium flame.

Max glanced at Damian, who shrugged and pointed to the bible. He licked his lips and stepped forward to begin the exorcism. The ghost froze and his gaze settled on the intruder. He snarled warningly.

"It's okay," the trainee said gently. "I'm here to help you move on to the next place."

It was silent for a heartbeat, then the spirit screamed, his mouth now large and wide. Max stumbled back against the wall as the apparition went berserk. "I think he wants us to go."

Damian laughed. "They always do."

The young priest grabbed his mentor and yanked him down. "Watch out!"

An entire rack of pots and pans rocketed over their heads and crashed into the walls behind them. They shielded their heads instinctively, but Max's feet began to slide on the floor as the wind picked up. He clutched the leg of the kitchen island to anchor himself. The ghost created another strong gust of wind, and the entire island hurtled to the right and smashed through the window. The men rolled across the floor with their backs toward the debris.

The spirit screeched again and slammed his fists to his sides. Simultaneously, the cooktop exploded behind him and flames shot into the air. Knives slammed into the wall beside them, and Max looked at Damian with wide eyes. The older priest raised his eyebrows. "Hopefully that is all the sharp objects in here."

A cleaver spiraled onto the floor between Max's legs.

He yelped and thrust the cross and bible in front of him. "I need to act fast, or this guy will flambé us and serve us to his ghostly little friends. Being a spitted roast is not my idea of a pleasant end."

Damian snorted. "Nor mine. I know where they stick that rod, and it's not pretty, my friend. Not pretty at all. But you have to face him head-on. Get to your feet and project the exorcism at him with power."

Max groaned and eyed the cleaver one last time. The spirit grew increasingly volatile, intensifying the wind and throwing anything he could. The dishes on the shelves rocked crazily against the glass-fronted cabinets. The doors swung open, and Max instinctively grabbed the top of the island, which had broken off, and raised it like a shield. They ducked and the crockery shattered against it. Glass exploded around them, and shards landed as far back as the wrecked window.

The young priest peered over the edge of the countertop and ducked again as a turkey carver embedded itself in the wood. Damian grabbed the makeshift shield and fixed Max with a firm look. "You can do this. I'll anchor you the whole time. When he runs out of things to throw, you can really focus on him. You're doing great, Max."

"Right. I'm merely trying to stay alive."

CHAPTER EIGHTEEN

Damian knelt and held fast to Max's leg as the young man stood. The firm grip anchored him against the ever-increasing wind, and the young priest cleared his throat and held the cross with one hand and the open bible in the other. The pages flipped wildly, and he closed his eyes to focus inward. *Come on, you know this prayer. You don't need the bible.*

He opened his eyes again. The ghost now wailed loudly and swirled the wind around them. *"Deus est creator. Deus est enim qui delevit. Benedicat sibi in orbem terrarum et hoc homine. Huc non pertinent. Fratremque vestrum in sanctificationem illius animae imaginem creantis eum renovatur..."*

The spirit lashed out, and bursts of energy scudded across the room in waves. Max stumbled but regained his footing. Damian nodded urgently. "Continue. He is not strong enough to hurt you at this point. He will try, but keep going."

The trainee nodded and repeated the prayer over and

over. He gave Damian the bible and held the cross with both hands, calling on the power of God to exorcise the spirit. *"Domine Omnipotens accipere eum in domum tuam. In nomine Patris et Filii et Spiritu Sancti."*

The entity rose from the floor, its near-translucent body vibrating. He hovered below the ceiling and gasped as rays of light burst from his chest. Max scrambled for cover. "Fucking shit, he's gonna blow!"

The two men lay flat behind the counter and covered their heads. This ghost, unlike the one in the cemetery, offered no words of wisdom or screams of anger. Instead, he growled loudly before exploding into a clear oozing mess that splattered from one side of the kitchen to the other.

The wind died immediately, and the burners' flames returned to normal. Max and Damian stood slowly, ooze dripping from their hats. The older priest looked at his suit and sighed in obvious relief. "He managed to miss my entire suit. Good job, dude."

Damian slapped the trainee's back, and his hand froze for a moment. When he raised it, strings of goo followed, and he grimaced. Max simply stood there with ooze dripping down his cheeks. Wordlessly, the young priest slid the cross into the leather pocket of Damian's coat. He removed the gloves and handed them over, slightly dazed from the whole occurrence.

Concerned, Damian asked, "You okay?"

Max swallowed and stared at the burn marks on the kitchen walls. "We really need to wear coveralls and goggles when we do these."

The pub was loud and boisterous. Music from the jukebox competed with the chatter around them. The only person who seemed to notice was Max, who slumped unhappily in his chair with his shoulders raised to his ears. Maps bobbed her head happily in time to the music, and Damian sipped his whiskey calmly. "It feels good to be here; like coming home."

"That's disturbing for a priest to say," Max remarked snidely

Maps glanced at him and laughed. "Oh, lighten up, you old stooge. Have a shot and relax. You aren't fighting demons right now."

Damian chuckled and raised his glass, taking a sip before anyone could respond to the silent toast. "How about you, Maps? How is business?"

She nodded around a huge bite of pizza. "Mmm, good. I actually have a lot of return clients and one new one. He's slightly odd, and I haven't figured him out yet. On the one hand, he might simply be weird, but on the other, he might be infected."

Damian tensed, a little curious now. "Does he have red eyes?"

Maps shrugged. "I don't know. He never removes his glasses, and it would be rude if I asked him to. He seems really nervous around me."

"Smart guy." Max chuckled drily.

She stuck her tongue out at him and dipped her pizza in ranch dressing. "He's not flirty and nervous like Max was when we first met."

The trainee straightened angrily. "That's not true. I simply wasn't used to derelicts like you, and wanted to make sure you wouldn't shank me or anything."

Maps pointed her plastic knife at him. "You can never be sure, can you? Anyway, I really don't think he's up to no good."

"How can you be sure?" Damian asked. "You should let me check him out."

"I appreciate that, Pops, but it's not necessary. I say that because everything he orders has to do with either food or the preparation of it. He asked for these ancient tart recipes, things Queen Victoria was fed, and all kinds of weird desserts. Unless he plans to attack someone with a crème brûlée, I think the world is safe."

Max rolled his eyes and glanced at Damian. "I'm pretty sure I could go the rest of my life without talking to another chef after today. In fact, if I had the choice, I would avoid all kitchens and food for eternity. I knew chefs could be testy assholes, but that guy had a serious issue."

Maps reached over and ruffled his hair, much to his dismay. "Aww, what's wrong, Maxie-poo? You get a bad chicken salad?"

He slapped her hand away and folded his arms.

Damian laughed and shook his head. "No, something way more awesome. Our man Max here did his first exorcism without my assistance—minus me making sure he didn't blow away in the wind. The ghost happened to be a chef. When we arrived, he was whistling to himself like a Muppet and chopping invisible vegetables."

She frowned. "What made him join the land of the dead?"

Damian tilted his head in thought as he sipped his whiskey. "At first we had no idea, since we actually stumbled on the house while we were out for a walk. When we got home, we did a little research, and it turns out he was a Michelin three-star chef from London. He liked to experiment in his multimillion-dollar kitchen—which is now a pile of rubble—before he took recipes into the restaurant. Apparently, his creativity got a little out of hand one day, thanks to a bottle of Scotch he left near the stove, and everything blew up in his face...literally."

Maps grimaced. "Yikes, that sucks. Did anyone else live there?"

Damian shook his head. "No, he was divorced, as so many in his profession are. I made a call to the real estate agent, who said they couldn't show the house because of the ghost. I told her that aside from some necessary repairs to the kitchen, they were good to go."

She wiped her hands and chin with a napkin. "Every time I tire of my chosen career, I remind myself how lucky I am to work with the living instead of the dead. I don't think I could handle the whole dramatic ghost thing. Seriously, they're dead! What do they have to whine about? Move on, please. I mean, what was his unfinished business —an unbaked souffle? People have real problems in this world."

Damian smirked. "That's true, although most of these spirits have no idea that they've died. There is the unfinished business part, but then there is the missed-the-bus kind. From what I've been taught, when a person dies, there is a limited window to move to the next place. Some of them are so confused that they end up missing that and are stuck in an in-between existence. They don't compute that no one talks to them. They don't compute that they aren't actually frying anything in that pan. They feel anger, rage, sadness, and mostly, fear. When we show up, they fear us. I don't know what they think we're there for, but they do everything they can to take us down."

Maps gulped her beer. "Yeah, well, the living can be that way too. Sometimes they let all their rage out on the people who try to help them. It's sad, really."

"It is," Max agreed. "Life is sad, and death is sad. Can't get away from it."

She startled suddenly. "Oh! Have you watched the news?"

"No, I've been a little busy," Damian said.

She grimaced and leaned forward. "Man, there have been some serious incursions lately. On top of that, Katie and her crew went back to hell and had themselves a jolly old fight. I'm talking bombs, fire, and troops running in and out. They showed video from the drones they sent in, and it was nuts. They hurt that big-ass demon pretty good, but a ton of them were injured too. Katie is okay, but one of their teammates—some huge guy—apparently bit it. At least, that's what the news said. It's been insane out there."

Damian frowned. "That's not good. I'll have to give her a call and make sure everything is kosher."

Maps exhaled loudly and gazed into the distance. "Shit is so wild out there. I mean, even *I* can tell it's getting worse."

Damian was interested in what she had to say. "How so?"

Maps shrugged. "I see infected people wherever I go. I

don't mean like in the 'I see dead people' kind of way either. There are literally red eyes everywhere—people in suits walking down the street, homeless blokes, protestors —the whole nine yards. And forget about the places I usually go. I'm in the minority, not having red eyes, and I now wear sunglasses so they can't identify me as quickly. I don't need anyone to grab me and try to put one of those things in me. No offense to your demons. I'm sure they're cool, but I don't want one. I like my alone time."

The older priest groaned and set his glass down. "This is what I'm talking about. When the mercs started disbanding and doing their own thing, there was more protection at the government level, but the everyday action decreased exponentially. There are no longer teams on every corner making sure the streets are safe. What they need is a better and bigger merc team here in London. They need boots on the ground to take these cells down, and eventually, you'll see fewer red eyes."

Maps grabbed a fry from Max's plate, ignoring his scowl. "You've got the ammunition. Why don't you create a group? With your connections, you could have the next Katie's Killers here in London. Then you could clean house."

Damian shook his head. "Sounds fantastic, but I'm not in that business anymore. There is only so much I can do within the limits of my current position with the church. I unfortunately have to follow the rules now. After the last incursion two days ago, I need to keep to the straight and narrow."

Maps wiggled her eyebrows and grinned. "Uh oh. What did you do two days ago? Broke the rules and took names?"

Max scoffed and folded his arms militantly. "More like locked me in a closet while he fought demons with a bunch of mercs. There were hundreds of them. I could have gotten in on the action, but no. I sat in a dusty old closet in the dark until he finally remembered he'd put me there."

"Poor Maximillian. Seriously though, he probably did you a favor. I've seen those bad boys in action, and it wouldn't have been as much fun as you thought. So, the higher-ups are pissed because you fought with the mercs?"

Damian wrinkled his nose scornfully. "Yes and no. Yes, because I shouldn't use weapons beyond my bible. My task was to exorcise those I could and get out of there. Of course, there was no way I could leave that team without pitching in. Then there was Max. The Wise Men wanted to see what he could do. I kind of defied them, feeling he wasn't ready for something of that magnitude, and stuck him in the closet instead."

Max slapped his hand on the table. "I *knew* there was more to it than what you told me. The Wise Men wanted me set free, and you were afraid I would die."

Maps nudged him. "Don't get too mad. That was actually really nice of him. I've read some of the secret artifact documents. They don't look fondly on priests when they break the rules. I'm sure that the people in charge—these Wise Men—are more than pissed."

Damian shrugged and glanced at Max, who relaxed a little. "So, tell me what's been big in the news besides incursions? Any new reality television on the tube?"

He changed the subject quickly, knowing she would launch into a diatribe against the latest *Bachelor, Dancing with the Stars,* and *Celebrity Rehab.* Damian knew that things with the church could go one of two ways. Either they would remedy his inability to follow directions by removing him completely, or they would permit him to do what he used to do. He had to believe he was too valuable to get rid of, and he wondered how long it would take until the second option took precedence.

Becoming a merc under their auspices would be both a curse and a blessing. He would do what he did before, which would be exhilarating, but he would still have to maneuver through the limitations of the church. Whether or not they wanted him to fight, it was an inevitable part of the job. He wouldn't argue if they finally embraced that fact.

CHAPTER NINETEEN

Back home that night, Damian made a beeline for his bedroom. He looked tired, and Max could tell he had a lot on his mind. Left to his own devices, the trainee meandered into the kitchen, served himself a huge bowl of lavender ice cream, and made a piping hot cup of tea. He smiled in anticipation and clicked the light off with his elbow, maneuvered through the darkened living room without mishap, and kicked his bedroom door shut behind him. His latest set of pajamas were a few weeks premature, but he didn't mind. The pants were covered in turkeys, and two eyes and a beak stared from the shirt.

Astaroth chuckled. *It's a good thing I couldn't give two shits about fashion. If I did, you'd burn all your clothes. Every single last pair of printed pajama pants would vanish in a flash of fire.*

Max smirked, climbed on the bed, and pulled the covers up. *Don't be jealous because I have legs to wear pants on.*

Touché, touché. The demon laughed loudly. *That was a good one. You're learning.*

The priest smiled and grabbed the remote. He had splurged a little on a flat-screen for his bedroom. Damian spent most of his time reading in the living room, and Max didn't want to bother his mentor when he watched television at night. He was hooked on the soaps, and it was non-negotiable that he stayed as current as possible. Originally, he'd watched because Damian was into them, but over time the older priest had shifted his focus to his books.

Max didn't know what the books were about, but whatever it was, he became completely engrossed in them. If Damian wanted him to know, he would tell him. Besides, Max completely understood the pull of books. He had once read seven books in only four days.

The sound of the fire being stoked caught Max's attention, and he crawled out of bed and opened the door. Damian sat in his usual chair. Max waved as his mentor looked at him. "Just wanted to say goodnight."

"Night, Maximus. See you in the morning."

Recognizing the dismissal, he closed the door and jumped back into bed. He dug his spoon into the ice cream and shivered slightly as the cold hit his tongue and the treat melted enticingly.

Astaroth groaned along with him. *You have turned me into a soap-opera-watching housewife with an obsession for ridiculous flavors of ice cream.*

Max chuckled. *I know, isn't it the best? I never thought I would like soaps, but hey, they catch my attention. It's a world I know nothing about. Do you think people really live like that?*

The demon snorted. *Maybe, but I hope not. They seem absolutely miserable all the time. It would be exhausting living in a constant dramatic battle with everyone around me.*

I feel like that's exactly what our life is like, minus the romance.

Astaroth exhaled a snarky breath. *My dear boy, you will never truly understand the meaning of drama until you have been caught up in a love triangle. It's exhausting and makes hell look like the fucking Caribbean.*

Max shrugged. *That's one drama I'll never have to worry about.*

He grabbed his mug and sipped the hot liquid. Astaroth coughed and made a fake gagging sound. *What in the world are you doing?*

What?

The demon groaned dramatically. *Why would you drink tea when you could have an exotic lavender-blended coffee? It would counter the sweetness of the ice cream but pair perfectly, with hints of that floral bouquet.*

Max frowned dismissively. *I like tea, and this one in particular with my ice cream. Besides, it's decaf, and I really don't want to drink coffee and be up all night. I'm trying to relax, not send my heart rate through the roof. Maybe we could try some decaf coffee blends.*

Are you absolutely out of your mind? Astaroth sputtered. *What kind of heathen do you take me for? No one drinks decaf because they appreciate the subtle hints of wonder in the bean. Next thing you know, we'll have a jar of instant coffee on the shelf and a carafe of fake-flavored creamer. Disgusting. You are* disgusting.

Sheesh, relax. I'm simply trying to relax after the exorcism today. I think, all in all, I did pretty well.

Astaroth cleared his throat. *I have to agree with you. I don't know if you would have been as spectacular on your own, but it was quick thinking to use the kitchen island counter as a shield for the two of you. However, I have to say that during the incursion, you were a hot mess. Did you really poke a demon in the eye with your finger?*

Max grimaced at the memory. *I hoped you hadn't noticed that. In the gym, I have the moves down, but I panic a bit out there.*

That happens. It means you aren't comfortable with the moves yet and they don't come naturally, but they will. All you have to do is get back into the gym, and we will work harder on everything.

Oh, boy, I'm so looking forward to more hard work in the gym.

The demon sniffed. *I'll ignore the sarcasm and focus on the new episode coming on.*

Max grinned and turned the volume up. He watched the recap of the week's episodes and started the show. As the opening scene rolled, he raised the spoon to his mouth but froze, and the ice cream plopped back into his bowl.

Astaroth gasped. *Oh, no, she did not. Are you kidding me? After all Troy did to get her out of hell, she cheats on him with Mr. Perfect Teeth? That is complete bullshit. They say demons are bad, but I think women have the ticket to pure evil.*

Max thumped his fist on the bed. *Not to mention that Troy lost his dang hand in a battle with one of the underlings below. He has one hand and is a hero, and she wants the flipping dentist? I don't get it.*

Wait! Pause and rewind. Yes, look at that.

The priest narrowed his eyes and focused on the still shot of the dentist turning toward the camera. He saw a distinct flash of red in his eyes. *Whoa. So either the actor is a demon in real life, or the dentist is infected. If he is infected, that means he's used a spell on her, and she didn't really choose him over Troy. Wow. That would be some shit.*

Astaroth clicked his tongue in disapproval. *Women are the strongest and toughest creatures on Earth, but these shows always make them fall for infected so easily. I truly believe that in the real world, she would have kung fu-chopped his perfect teeth down his throat.*

Max nodded, spooning ice cream into his mouth without taking his eyes from the screen. *Hell, yeah, she would have. Now Troy will be heartbroken, but only until he figures this all out.*

Which will take at least twelve episodes. The demon groaned. *That's two and a half weeks of these two bumbling idiots drinking champagne. I hope we are right, though. Otherwise, the studio might need to investigate the actor.*

The priest shook his head. *I think no matter what, she would have picked the hot, less intelligent guy.*

Astaroth wasn't so sure. *I don't know. I think she's got a good head on her shoulders, and Troy isn't bad-looking. I think you might be surprised at how quickly she takes him back. He's smart, successful, and even with one hand, runs a multi-million-dollar company.*

Max leaned back and continued the show, feeling a sense of home as he and his demon argued over the characters. He was finally comfortable, as if he were where he was supposed to be.

Damian sipped hot coffee as the blaze crackled wildly in

the fireplace. He settled into his chair, pulled the blanket over his shoulders, and grabbed one of the journals from the stack. Although he always started out with a pile, he rarely made it past the first one most days. Things had changed since he had first arrived and had all the time in the world to do what he wanted. He worked and had missions at that point, and they sucked the energy right out of him.

Before he could open the journal, his phone rang. He set his cup down and paused, biting the inside of his lip. *It's probably the Secretary, calling to bitch me out even worse than she already has. I should ignore it and call her back tomorrow.*

Ravi wasn't so sure. *I don't know, Pops. What if there is an emergency? You don't want her droid showing up on your doorstep. We aren't ready for that next-level sci-fi shit.*

Damian groaned and capitulated, knowing she was right. He turned the phone and smiled the minute he saw Katie's name. He pressed Answer, and the screen flipped to the video chat feature. Her calm face appeared, drawing his smile wider. He raised an eyebrow, noting her slightly higher cheekbones and longer hair. Clearly, Pandora still put the time in to tweak her body.

"My dear Katie, I was just talking about you earlier today," Damian began happily as he fiddled to focus his camera.

She smiled. "I thought I felt an itch on my nose."

"What?"

Katie laughed. "My mom always used to say that whenever someone was talking about me, my nose would itch."

Damian chuckled. "You must have been the talk of the town during allergy season."

They shared a comfortable laugh. Katie drew a deep breath and looked directly into the camera. "How are you? I feel like we don't talk enough."

He nodded. "I agree, we don't. Nonetheless, I am still here. There was an incursion the other day, and I ended up working with a merc team. It felt like old times. One of the mercs was from New York—Charlie."

She seemed surprised. "Yeah, I remember Charlie—hell of a warrior. He left right after Incursion Day. I didn't know he had hopped across the pond. Good for him. I like it. And as for you working with them, I'm sure you kicked serious ass. We miss you here."

"I miss you too." Damian sighed, knowing that was the truth. "I think I'm doing valuable work here, though. I heard about your battles in hell. How is that going?"

Katie shrugged. "Oh, you know. Faking deaths, killing demons, blowing the legs off Moloch. All the normal stuff. It's definitely hot down there."

Damian glanced at the book in his hand. "Hey, do you think I could talk to Pandora? The only thing is, I would like to talk to her about something private on her end. If you switch, can she make it so you can't hear? No offense, but it's her business to tell you."

His friend grew quiet for a moment, and Damian could see by the look on her face she was talking to Pandora. "She said she can make it happen. Hold on one second."

Katie's image shimmered slightly, and her features changed enough that he knew he was talking to Pandora. The demon put her finger up and concentrated for a moment before exhaling slowly. "Okay, she is muted.

What's up, Damian? It's not the same here without your holiness prodding at my evil fucking soul."

Damian laughed. "I know. Who will keep you good now? Though I think you may be in more control of that than you let on."

Pandora rolled her eyes. "Please. Bitchin' demon through and through. So, what's this super-secretive shit you got going on?"

"Well, I think I have something of yours."

The demon sputtered. "Oh, priest, don't you know I lost my virginity centuries ago? That shit is gone and buried."

He laughed loudly. "I have a feeling that couldn't be found even in the deepest depths of hell, but it's not what I'm talking about."

Damian opened the book and read one of the witty comments out loud. "If the devil doesn't want us, you dick-snarfing repugnant imbecile, then why are we chilling in hell?" Damian looked at her and blinked. "Shall I go on?"

Pandora's face deadpanned. "No. Look, I know you probably have a lot of questions about this. Anyone would, but you'll have to wait for answers. I need to trust that you'll keep that book secret, at least for a little while longer."

He frowned at the idea of lying to Katie, but he could understand to a degree. "I'll make you a deal. I'll keep the secret, but whatever you're hiding, when it finally comes out, you let me ask whatever questions I want. You will answer them truthfully and honestly. This is a big secret, my dear, something that Katie should be told, but I know it's your place to tell her. What do you say? Do we have a deal?"

Pandora pursed her lips and narrowed her eyes, staring hard at Damian. "Priest, you drive a goddamn hard bargain, but shit, why-fucking-not? You have a deal, but don't jerk me around on this one."

Damian put the book down. "I will not jerk you around."

She snickered. "Good, 'cause God is watching those hands, priest."

CHAPTER TWENTY

The sun blazed through the windows as Damian stood in the kitchen, humming happily to himself. He had spoken to both Katie and Pandora the night before and had slept without his mind racing. The kettle whistled loudly, and he poured the water into his drip coffee container. Still humming snatches of a song, he stirred in sugar and milk, took a sip, and smiled as he cleaned the dishes. It was a beautiful sunny day, and the temperature soared above average, already up to sixty degrees.

The seasons were changing, and Damian loved the contrasts. Vegas basically looked the same all year round, which was his only complaint. It got cold there, sure, but only at night, and there were no trees to change color, no big snowfalls, and no seasonal anticipation of the holidays. The rest was great. Family, friends, and action always close by.

He selected a grape from a bunch on the counter and popped it in his mouth. *Shall we enjoy this beautiful morning?*

Ravi yawned. *Is this different than any other morning? And what's with the super-cheerful attitude? It's giving me the willies.*

Damian chuckled as he walked toward the door. *I wasn't stressed about anything last night. It was probably the most dreamless sleep I've had in years. I knew Max was on the right track, I knew Katie was safe and kicking ass, and I didn't let the cardinal stuff get me in a foul mood.*

I still wish you'd sleep in once in a while, she grumbled. *I know I can stay asleep, but with all these happy emotions poking at me, I had to wake up. I couldn't chance a dream about unicorns and fucking ponies.*

Maybe a little rainbow sunshine happiness will melt some of that doom and gloom off your bones.

If you haven't noticed, demons don't really like sunshine. We also tend to eat anything that could possibly bring happiness, although I stick to a vegetarian diet when I'm in hell. I don't do live animals, and they don't like to cook stuff.

Damian wrinkled his nose in disgust. *Strange, considering you could literally walk out your door and barbeque over the lava pits.*

Ravi sniffed. *Speaking of old cooked meat, you hear from Rose?*

Damian shivered. *That analogy was disgusting, and no, I haven't. I hope she comes outside this morning. I'd like to talk to her about a few things. Maybe I can sharpen that idea of me helping her fight the demon.*

He unlocked the door, whistling cheerfully, and stepped over the threshold. Something whizzed past his head and thwacked into the doorframe. Slowly, he turned to stare at a butcher knife impaled in the wood. His eyes flashed, and he swiveled to look across the courtyard. Rose rushed into her apartment and slammed the door behind her.

Ravi gasped. *Oh no, she didn't. That crazy old bat almost knifed you in the middle of this courtyard. Fuck holding back.*

Damian gritted his teeth. "That's exactly what I thought."

He yanked the knife out of the door and strode across the courtyard, pausing only to set his coffee mug on the table. Rose's door was locked, and he growled loudly and banged on the wood. "Ms. Rose. You forgot something…in my front door. Open up. I only want to talk."

A whimper and a low snarl sounded from inside. Rose was obviously trying to fight the demon. Damian jiggled the handle again and glanced furtively around to check that no one was watching. *Give me a boost of strength.*

Ravi giggled. *You got it.*

The priest stepped back and kicked hard to slam the door off its hinges. It slid down the hall and fell in an eddy of dust, and he could see the particles floating in the rays coming from the open door. His eyes checked every shadow and crevice of the hallway. He knew she was in there but not exactly where.

Damian cleared his throat and tapped the knife against the wall. "Ms. Rose, come out. I want to talk to your demon. I have an offer for him."

A small growl issued from the living room. Carefully, he walked down the hallway, alert for more knives or other lethal missiles. He passed the study and smiled sadly. It was obvious that the demon-induced stress had left Rose unable to really clean anything, and she had always been so neat and tidy that the current neglect was heartbreaking. It was another reminder that the church had abandoned her, leaving the poor, sweet old woman to battle the demon on her own regardless of the cost, which might even be her life.

The priest paused in the entrance to the living room, unsure where she was. "Rose, why don't you sit on the couch? We can talk."

A deep, menacing voice responded, "I'm not Rose."

"No, of course not. Why don't you tell me your name?"

Damian turned and saw Rose's red eyes flashing from the corner. The demon growled and hissed loudly, but the priest simply sighed, shook his head, and marched over to her. "I had planned to do this nicely, but I guess you won't let me."

He grabbed the old lady tightly by the arm and held the knife in front of her face. Her demon growled loudly and blinked wildly at the blade. Damian dragged her to the chair and thrust her into it. He held the knife to her face and leaned in close, his eyes flashing red. "If I were you, I wouldn't move. It's obvious Rose isn't here anymore, at least not in the front. I don't have a problem releasing her soul and sending you back to hell. I know you want to be here in this body."

The demon shut Rose's mouth and gritted her teeth. He tried to shift her gaze to the right, but Damian grabbed her face with his other hand and forced the beast to make eye contact. "Give her back. This is your only warning. Let Rose take control of her body."

The demon looked maliciously at him and began to spit and snarl. *"Muyt esaeu suzor scum. I lizz nid esaeun entrails aeuq oth aoq yaz maen girrabbi."*

Damian narrowed his eyes. "Now, that's rude. You know I can't understand that." He grabbed her by the throat and squeezed. "English."

The fiend laughed menacingly. "Fuck you, human scum. I will rip your entrails out and eat them for dinner. You can't do anything to me. Your precious church forbids it."

The priest then squeezed tighter, shutting the demon up. "Do you see shackles on my wrists?"

He loosened his grip, and the demon coughed. "You will burn in the fires of hell, just like the rest of your meatsack kind. Lucifer will wear your skins as clothes, and your souls will forever roast in Moloch's fireplace."

Damian sighed and poked the knife far enough into the demon for him to wince. "Shut your fucking mouth, demon. You let her back, or you won't have a soul to go back to hell. You think I don't know that you can be killed here on Earth?"

Ravi cleared her throat. *You should let me have a go at him. Maybe I can help.*

Damian eased the knife back. *You can speak to him? I thought—*

She cut him off. *It doesn't really matter what you thought at this moment, does it? You want me to talk to him or not? I can't promise it will do any good. I don't quite have the fear factor your Katie does, but I'm more than some low-level demon. He will know this. It will be up to him whether he fears me or not.*

The priest studied Rose and glimpsed the sweetness under the terror. *All right, give it a shot.*

Ravi breathed deeply, calmed herself, and pushed her awareness into the helpless woman. She spoke in demon so Damian couldn't understand. *S'es ona esaeu* doing *yiz? Chq yiz laezor kae. Ya* priest *gaeaz raeq k'oes xes ya* rules *aem ya khunkh aen oresaera ahza maen yoq zoqqabbi. Sa lizz zota zuna esaeu gaer'q zota iq xoyt qae sazz.*

Rose's demon went silent for a moment before he laughed again. "I don't fear you, bitch. You have no power here. You were cast away like the others. I will do as I please."

Damian scowled, wondering what he meant by that. Ravi snarled, *Believe me, you are messing with the wrong fucking priest. If you don't bring Rose back up, he will kill you both.*

"He cannot kill me." The fiend smirked. "I will simply come back for a new body, and then I will find you and kill you myself."

Ravi growled again and pushed her anger into Damian. He squeezed the demon harder. *It doesn't seem to be working.*

She shushed him. *I need to think. What are all demons afraid of? Wait, that's it.* Ravi took another deep breath and thrust in once more. *He may not be able to kill you, but he is kin to one who would not think twice of sending you to nothingness.*

The demon snorted. "What? Is he friends with Gabriel?"

Ravi smirked. *No, even better than that. One all demons fear. Shall I say her name? I think I will.*

She whispered in a way that pierced the air, filling them all with fear. The echoes of Lilith's name dribbled into the demon's head, and Ravi could feel him pull back. She switched to demon again. The priest listened, waiting for any sign of success. Rose's eyes were still bright red, and her breathing was heavy and fast.

Ravi pulled out of the body and shivers rippled through

Damian. *When I tell you, I want you to let her go,* she said quietly

Damian frowned. *Are you sure?*

Positive. I don't want her to come back with your hand around her neck. You will scare the ever-loving shit out of her. Okay, on my count. One...two...let go!

The priest released his hold and jumped back in case she attacked. He watched as her eyes closed and her head slumped forward. His chest twisted painfully, and he wondered if he had somehow killed the old woman. *Is she—*

No, Ravi whispered. *Wait a moment.*

Damian could still see her breathing, but she sat entirely motionless. He leaned forward, trying to see her face as his finger pressed lightly on her arm. Suddenly, Rose's head raised and she gasped and lifted her hand to her chest. Bewildered, she looked around the room, her eyes fading slowly from bright red to brown. She blinked several times at the closed curtains.

Rose pointed at them. "Can you open those?"

He nodded and pulled the curtains, and the light spilled into the room. Still holding the knife, Damian waited for her to speak. Her gaze settled on the blade and she clasped her hand over her mouth and shook her head as tears formed in her eyes. He put the knife down hastily. "I am not here to hurt you, Rose."

She sniffled, shook her head, and patted his arm. "No, I know you aren't. I remember the knife. Oh, good Lord in Heaven, I am so sorry about that. He was so strong. He wouldn't let me eat or sleep, and finally, he took over. I was too weak to fight him. I tried desperately, but all I could do was shift his aim."

Damian chuckled. "I appreciate that. It almost hit me."

Rose let her hands drop into her lap and sighed. "What a fight. I'm so sorry, Damian. I don't know why they don't put me out. It's dangerous now."

He shushed her and gathered her hands in his. "We will fight for your life together. Wait here. I'll fix you a nice cup of tea. How do you take it?"

"One sugar and a splash of milk. Thank you."

Damian searched the kitchen until he found the teapot. The place was a disaster, so he cleaned two teacups while he waited for the kettle to boil. He was a little startled that things had happened the way they had but relieved. Using Ravi to push the demon back was the best he could do at that point. The church wouldn't allow any more.

When the tea was ready, he handed her a cup and sat in the chair opposite her. He noticed that her hands shook as she lifted it to her lips and took a sip. She closed her eyes as the warmth refreshed her. "Leave it to an Englishwoman to take tea over water after days without anything."

Damian chuckled. "I think we have the demon under control for now, but eventually you'll have to let someone do something about this. Your life is too precious to be taken over by this beast."

Rose nodded and stared out the window. "I don't know what you did, but he is deep inside and terrified as hell."

CHAPTER TWENTY-ONE

When the conversation dwindled, Damian covered her with a blanket and set to work in her kitchen. He did the dishes, threw the trash out, and mopped the floor. As he worked, he found all the dangerous chemicals and tossed them out as well. He didn't know how desperate the demon was to stay away from Lilith and wanted to avoid him forcing her to harm herself. He found potatoes, leftover chicken, carrots, celery, and spices and prepared a pot of hot soup. She needed something that would nourish her body quickly and help her regain her strength.

Rose was thankful for his help since she was too weak to do it on her own. After he served her on a tray in the living room, he ran out to the local hardware store for new hinges. Carefully and quietly, he hung her door back where it belonged. He had kicked it down, after all. She smiled as he tested it. "You are pretty strong to kick that door down."

Damian chuckled. "I had a bit of help."

She rubbed her head absently. "Was that the other voice I heard? Was that your demon?"

"Yes, her name is Ravi."

Rose smiled. "Tell her thank you as well."

He took the tray from her, helped her up, and guided her into her room. "I think you should get some sleep. I will come back and check on you later, or I'll send Max over. The soup is in the fridge if you want more."

She stretched out on the bed and Damian pulled the covers up. "Thank you, Damian. You truly are a messenger of God." She put her hand on his and smiled.

He smiled and patted her hand, then flipped the light off. Before he could leave, Rose called him. "Yes?" He paused in the doorway.

"I wouldn't call Ravi a demon. She is also known as Ameretat."

His eyes focused on the floor as he considered this. "But Ameretat was a man in folklore."

Rose laughed and shifted to a more comfortable position. "Only because a man wrote it."

Damian nodded and closed her bedroom door. Ravi was silent as he returned home, saying nothing about what Rose had revealed. He stopped at the table and picked up his coffee mug, grimacing at how cold it was. *Oh, well, it was for a good cause, I suppose.*

The priest hurried inside and set his cup in the sink before retrieving his two fallen angel books from the safe. He looked at his normal seat by the fire and shook his head. "I need more concentration than that."

Within minutes, he'd donned his coat, grabbed his umbrella, and headed to the local church library six blocks from where he lived. He had discovered it on his second day, but he found it too quiet for him. Now, though, he needed the silence to allow his head to absorb all that had happened.

When he entered the library, the sound of the door opening echoed through the silent reading area. The nun at the front desk looked up from her book and smiled kindly. She had seen him a couple of times and knew he was permitted entry. He nodded a greeting and found a table tucked away from the others at the back. The people who frequented the library rarely paid any attention to anyone else, but he wanted to be safe.

The atmosphere was much like the church he had grown up in—serious and silent, with ornate fixtures and solemn furnishings. He hadn't brought Max there yet, but he planned to. The only thing he didn't like was that it seemed to put Ravi in a very quiet coma-like state. She was almost asleep and rarely paid attention to what he said. He wasn't sure why it had that effect on her, but it didn't seem to hurt her.

The demon cleared her throat and yawned. She had heard his thoughts. *To answer you, I struggle with how holy this place is, so I go into hibernation. Wake me when you're done.*

Damian narrowed his eyes. For some reason, he didn't believe her. She had been in some of the holiest churches on Earth and hadn't reacted that way. He had a hard time believing that a library, church-owned or not, was holier than those. Nonetheless, he let her sleep and focused on his task.

He settled and retrieved the books from his well-worn bag but made no move to open them until he had taken a good look around. There were only four or five other priests in the library, and none paid him any heed. They tended to notice him more when it was full, but only because of the clothes he wore. He didn't look like a typical priest, and several Catholics came there to study. They frowned on those who didn't follow the church culture to a T, although Damian didn't care. After one look, they quickly put him out their minds.

He shrugged his jacket off, draped it on the chair behind him, and rolled his shoulders. Unsure where to start, he shrugged and picked up the book Lilith had annotated. He had already started it, so why not continue? He flipped through the pages again to where he had left off but thought better of it. The words in the corners and sides weren't really appropriate for a church setting.

The next chapter was titled, *Walking on the Earth.* Next to that Lilith had snarked, *As opposed to swimming on the Earth? Flying on the Earth? Idiot.* Damian smirked and turned the page, trying to ignore the notes and focus on the text. When he finished, he already knew the comments would be harsh. Lilith cussed the writer up one side and down the other, making her feelings clear.

Please, we eat only berries and drink wine? I mean, sure, give me some fucking booze, but berries? Try fucking double cheeseburgers and donuts, bitch.

Damian stifled a laugh with his hand over his lips. On the entire right side of the page, Pandora had played her own game of connect the dots. The words were strung together by etched vines shaped like an erect penis with two overly large dangling testicles. At the bottom the note read, *Short and stubby, this is how I think this writer walks around. His balls make him walk like he has a shoe up his ass, or maybe his fucking head.*

He closed the book slightly as a priest walked by and nodded a greeting. Damian smiled back and waited for him to pass before resuming. He read through the rest of the chapter and shook his head. *She must have had no friends at that point. I hope she never met this poor soul.* He flipped the page, and two folded pieces of paper dropped into his lap. His eyes narrowed, and he closed the book and placed it on the table. The old paper looked fragile and scorched at the edges. Carefully, he unfolded both letters and smoothed them carefully on the desk in front of him.

A furtive glance assured him that no one was paying him any attention. Damian hunched over the table and ran his finger across the papers. Strange energy seemed to rise from the first. He jerked his hand back and cleared his throat, feeling Ravi wake. She must have felt the same surge as he had. For some reason, Damian had the oddest feeling that he shouldn't read it, but it was too conspicuous not to.

Finally, he slipped his gloves on under the table and stretched his fingers to loosen the cold leather a little. He held the first letter in his lap and covered the second with the book.

Dearest New Wife,

It has been 3567 very long and chilly days in the caverns. Your robes still lay across the throne of bones, awaiting your return. At first, I must admit, I was angry. However, after torturing a few thousand souls and feasting on their skins, I began to feel better. I remembered that you have a free soul, and this "vacation" you have taken is only temporary. I need to let you spread your scales and do what you must to be happy.

Nonetheless, you are the Queen, and as such, you have certain responsibilities. Your brother has picked up the slack, but let's be honest. He is nowhere as cruel and evil as you are. You must return to the inner rings immediately. I know you like to defy my rule, but it is imperative that you do not thwart me. You know my wrath can be harsh and swift, and my love for you is stronger. Do not be fooled, though. I will do what is necessary to secure your presence. We took the unholy vow, which means you are the only one who can rule as Queen for eternity.

You have betrayed this and abandoned me. Come back. I will send the Leviathan for you if you do not respond. I have been told you are somewhere in Korea, and I will kill every human in my path. Be warned.

Yours in Darkness,

Lucifer

Damian's mouth dropped open for a moment, and he chuckled. The handwriting seemed to be in some sort of red liquid, thinner than ink and soaked into the paper. He removed a glove and rubbed the page between his fingers, considering the texture. It felt strange, as if it were made of some sort of hide.

Human, Ravi said abruptly. *Human skin.*

He dropped the letter on the desk and wiped his hand on his shirt. Once he'd cleared his throat and replaced the glove, he picked the other page up carefully. Thankfully, it appeared to be some sort of thick paper. This letter was considerably shorter.

Lucifer,

I told you my time there would be limited, yet you insisted on *pulling your masculine bullshit and tried to control me. I do not care that you have a title. You will not force me into what I do not wish to do. Like I told you before, my time with you is limited. I will return soon to run the kingdom, and we can discuss our future. You were aware from the moment I took the throne that my wings were still there, waiting to be brought to reckoning. I do not do well in your kind of hell.*

Please walk my precious Cerberus. I will arrive when I please. If you send your Leviathan, I will make a mockery of it. I promise you.

XO... Lilith

The priest's eyes widened, and he folded the letters quickly and shoved them into the pocket with his cross. He sat in silence, completely stunned that he had just read what amounted to love letters between Lucifer and Lilith. That was something he definitely needed to keep to himself. And what did she mean by wings?

CHAPTER TWENTY-TWO

Damian struggled to assimilate all the information he'd received that day. He tried desperately to get Ravi to talk to him, but she either gave him one-word answers or didn't respond. After several hours of trying to hide his frustration in the quiet library, he slammed the fallen angels book closed and shoved it in his bag.

He tapped his fingers on his thigh for a moment and considered ways to shift Ravi from her silent mode. *You know, I was thinking. My bag is pretty old, and I could possibly use a replacement. You wouldn't happen to know a shop where I could find one, would you?*

She perked up immediately. *Shopping? Did I hear that you need to go shopping? Has hell finally frozen over after all these millennia?*

Damian chuckled. *Calm down. It's just a bag.*

Ravi giggled. *Actually, I know the perfect place. It's been there for a very long time and has some of the best and most fashionable custom bags for a man like you.*

I'm not sure what 'a man like me' means, but okay. Where are we going?

The demon was shamelessly excited. *House of Fraser. They opened their first shop in 1849, selling finery in Glasgow, and now have a huge store in London.*

Damian gathered his things and left the library. *Just so you know, I am considering a new bag. That doesn't mean I'll go nuts and buy one, but I will be straight and honest with you. I will not wear a man purse. I want something similar to the one I have now; something classic, and I want it to last thirty years like this one has.*

Ravi chuckled. *What you refer to is actually called a Murse, and don't worry, I don't want you to embarrass me. No small shoulder bags for you. I won't even make you look at the ones that go around your waist.*

He cringed at the thought. *I appreciate that. It's not really my style, although I'm not sure I really have a defined style. I like to think of myself as exotic.*

She laughed loudly as they climbed into a cab. *I don't think "exotic" came to my mind, but okay, we'll go with it.*

They arrived, and Damian was relieved to see it was a larger department store like a Macy's back home. They wandered through until they found the bags section.

As they meandered, happily distracted by the different styles, he decided it was time for him to ask a few questions. *Let me ask you something. Do you like hell? Is it homey and comfortable for you?*

Ravi scoffed. *Please. It's hot as balls, and there are no cushions on anything. The food is terrible. You can't relax because of all the shrieking and moaning. It's a hideous place. I tried to make my house there comfortable, but it was pointless. I now spend as much time topside as possible.*

Damian nodded and ran his hand across a leather bag. *How long have you been a demon? I mean, from what Rose says, you are more than a demon, but you have yet to confirm that.*

Ravi sighed. *I am not Ameretat, although the thought is sweet. I* am *related to her in a long succession I knew nothing about until after death, but I am not a fallen angel. I merely know a lot of them.*

Before your death? Damian asked.

She cleared her throat with obvious discomfort. *I guess it's time I let you in on my secrets. Especially if I'll be stuck with you for a while. I was a human many, many years ago, born and raised in the new Baton Rouge. It was a time of excess for many, not excluding myself. I did not know my mother, and my father never spoke of her. He owned a large shipping company and was very rich, and I spent my days traveling the world, seeing the sights, and doing whatever I wanted. Mine was a life without lack. I partied and danced the nights away in Paris, London, Egypt, and the islands, and had many lovers but only one true love. My life was what every woman of that time wished theirs could be.*

Damian listened closely. *Did you have a family?*

Ravi went quiet for a moment. *No. No family of my own. When my father decided he wanted to pass the company on to me, I realized that everything would have to change. I wasn't happy about that.*

He was shocked. *I don't mean to be surprised, but I assumed you were a demon created in hell like so many of the others. I didn't realize you were a trapped soul, damned there for living a less than godly life during your human time on Earth.*

She chuckled. *I wish it were that simple. Sure, I didn't live the godliest life, but I wasn't a bad person. I fed the hungry, shared my wealth, cared for others, and did good deeds. I tithed, and I gave godly advice to others. But when it came down to it, I had no choice but to enter hell when I died. There was no option for me to even linger on Earth as a spirit.*

Damian stared at a bag without really seeing it. *I don't understand. I know we don't have a choice in our destiny once we have died, but you make it sound predetermined.*

Ravi groaned. *I really don't want to talk about this yet. I made a wrong choice in life, the last one I ever made. That, coupled with my family heritage, predetermined my future in the fiery pits of hell. I was not sent there as a common demon, but to me, there is no real difference. Hell is hell.*

Damian nodded, surprised by the surge of sadness he sensed in her. *I suppose it is, for those who don't want to be there. Whether you are in chains or on a couch, none of it is the preferred scenario. I do feel sorry for you, and I hate to say it that way. You lived what sounds like a magnificent life. You saw the world at a time when it was only a shadow of what it is today. Were you young when you passed?*

I was in my late twenties. Now, of course, it would be considered very young to have died. But again, this isn't the time or place for that conversation. I think I have given enough of myself to the wagging tongues.

Am I a wagging tongue?

Ravi laughed. *No, it's an expression. I used to hear my aunt say it all the time when I was alive. The gossips, the old biddies who liked to tell everyone's business. That's probably why I am so good at privacy now. I had a lot of practice as a human. I was pretty much the same girl alive that I am dead, only in hell I have scales. Dreadful things, and they fucking itch.*

Damian wanted to press further. He wanted to know who she was and why she'd been predetermined for hell. He began to ask a question, but Ravi had already changed the subject. She gasped and pushed his attention to the right.

Look at that bag. It's exactly what I had in mind. Sturdy, with lots of pockets. You can lock it, but it's still soft to the touch. Brown leather with thick stitching, so you'll have it for a very long time, just like the hobo sack you carry now.

The priest frowned at his bag. *Hey, this thing has been through the wringer. It has seen serious things during our time together.*

Ravi maintained an even tone. *Mmm. So, have I, but you won't find me wrinkly and worn.*

Damian rolled his eyes and picked the bag up. It definitely had a more fashionable flair, but he liked it, which surprised him. He seldom liked what Ravi chose. Like the suit, though, she had managed to grab his attention with that one. It was sturdy, too, and he thought he could store a good number of weapons in the thing. A latched leather-lined pouch on the front would be perfect for his cross when he didn't wear his trench.

He knew the demon had distracted him on purpose. While he wanted badly to delve into her background, she was determined to end the conversation. She had revealed more than he'd expected, so he decided it would do for now. And she was right about one thing—they had plenty of years ahead of them, so he had time to discover more. There was something deeply hidden, something bigger than being related to a fallen angel. It was significant enough that she wanted to hide it from him at any cost.

With the current state of the war, any secret about demons and angels could be the key to victory. He hoped that hers didn't impact the conflict because he wasn't sure how he would handle it if it did. Katie had been created to handle Pandora, but he was not equipped for anything remotely close to their relationship. The secrets nagged at him, and God knew he held his fair share of them. Between his demon, Pandora, and the cardinal, he was about as full of secrets as one man could get.

CHAPTER TWENTY-THREE

Damian opened the front door of the house and entered with a large paper bag. He closed it and tossed his house keys on the side table. The place was chilly, but he wanted to square his things away before he made another fire. He placed his old bag on the dining room table and the new one beside it.

He whistled intermittently as he removed the books from of old bag and dumped the pens and loose papers. One by one, he stationed the items neatly in his new bag, even discovering a hidden inside pocket where he could keep things he didn't want visible.

The fallen angels book would fit easily, making it the perfect hidey-hole for it when he was on the move. *Well, it looks like you made another fantastic choice.*

Ravi was smug. *I told you I was good at this stuff. Now all I have to do is get you to invest in new boots, and we will be on the right track.*

He looked defensively at his footwear. *These will do for now. They aren't even worn yet.*

She groaned theatrically. *Yeah, yeah. I guess I can't be too picky. I got you farther than I thought I would.*

Damian returned the books to the safe and hung his new bag in the closet. Ravi protested. *Do you mean to tell me you'll hide a beautiful leather satchel that you just paid twenty-five-hundred dollars for in the deep, dark recesses of your dungeon closet? Oh, no. No! I cannot allow this.*

He muttered and removed it, then walked to a dining room chair, and hung it over the back. The demon wasn't pleased and, conceding defeat, he hung it on a hook on the wall. *Better?*

She sniffed. *I can live with that.*

The priest smirked and removed the letters from his jacket pocket. Quickly, he returned to the safe and slid them into the fallen angels book, and after a short hesitation, he locked the safe and opted to pursue his search another night. Needing the distraction of human contact, he knocked on Max's door. When he didn't get a response, he knocked again and waited, finding it hard to believe the trainee would be asleep at that hour of the day. Finally, he creaked the door open and peeked inside.

Max wasn't in his room, and his bed was made. Damian scratched his head in thought and shut the door, then meandered through the dining room to the kitchen. Everything was spotless, and the young priest was nowhere to be found.

Ravi sniffed. *I smell him and his demon, so he is here somewhere. Maybe he discovered that closets are comfortable after all.*

See what you did to the kid? You damaged him for the rest of his life.

Damian rolled his eyes. *I did no such thing. If anyone damaged him, it was him. He's the clumsiest person I have ever met in my life. No motor skills at all.*

She snorted. *Maybe he will grow into them.*

He chuckled as he grabbed a grape and tossed it into the air, then caught it deftly in his mouth. *I saw his shoes on the stoop when I came in, so he is either here somewhere or is wandering the streets of London barefoot.*

Ravi grimaced. *As much as I love this city, I would not advise that.*

Just then, a loud crash sounded upstairs, followed by Max yelling and groaning. Damian looked at the ceiling with wide eyes and rushed to the stairs. He raced up them two at a time and swung around the wall, taking the corner fast. At the door to the training room, he stopped. Ravi tried to hide a laugh. *Oh my.*

Max hung upside down, his shirt over his face. He had managed to somehow get his foot caught in one of the full-sized practice dummies and now swayed back and forth, his head hitting the plastic leg.

Damian shook his head in disbelief. "How in God's name did you get yourself into that predicament?"

The young man lifted his shirt from his face. "I kicked the damn—I mean, dang—thing and somehow got stuck. Then it tipped over and swept me right off my feet."

His foot slipped, and he hit the floor at a ninety-degree angle with his back flat but his sock still trapped. All Damian could do was laugh as he walked over and pulled. Max tried to pull with him, but it only tangled the material more firmly in the plastic, and the older man struggled to hold back his laughter. "Hold still. You can't— Stop pulling or I'll leave you like this."

Finally, Damian simply yanked the trainee's foot free. "You need to make sure there is supervision when you train. Apparently, it's more dangerous than fighting demons."

Max pushed to his feet and straightened his shirt, frowning at a hole near the hem. "Hey, I had some serious momentum going there. That thing attacked me."

His mentor regarded him in stunned silence for a moment before laughter overwhelmed him. He pushed the dummy with one finger, and it fell and bounced across the floor. "Oh, sure, this seems like a real mean one. Maybe we should get some rope and tie this bad boy up. We wouldn't want him attacking anyone else. We live here, and he could kill us in our sleep. I'm glad you tamed the beast, though. You're a real hero."

The young man faked a laugh and yanked his towel off the bench. "You don't know what I go through. You had an entire team of mercs to train you when you started out. I have you—and you're lost in books most of the time—and my demon. He's an asshole most days, but at least he helps me."

Damian smirked. "Oh, yeah, he came running straight to your aid when the killer plastic man attacked you."

Max frowned. "I guess it's not his fault I have no coordination. At least the dummy was there. I might have gone straight through the window otherwise. You would have found me in the courtyard with crazy Ms. Rose trying to drag me back to her lair."

"Oh, I don't think she'll be much of a problem anymore," he responded cheerfully. "At least, not for a while. She had a bit of a meltdown earlier, and I had to scare her demon into the recesses of her soul. Hopefully, it stays there for a while."

His companion raised an eyebrow in surprise. "Does that explain the shards of wood on the doorstep and the hole in our doorframe?"

Damian exhaled a long breath and shrugged. "That it does, but don't ask. It was a wild ride. In the meantime, you are tackling the villains at our backs."

Max's face dropped, and the older man smiled and draped his arm around his shoulder and shook him gently. "Hey, we all get attacked by an inanimate object at some point in our training. Luckily, I was here to save the day."

"Really?"

Damian shook his head. "No, you are definitely the first. Go ahead and take a shower, get dressed, and come downstairs. I know this little place that serves tapas and amazing coffee. I think both you and your demon will enjoy it. Sound good?"

Max nodded as Damian walked down the hall. The young priest flipped the lights off and rolled his eyes at the dummy. "Fucking mannequin."

His mentor hopped down the steps, his grin wide. "Language!"

Exasperated, Max threw his head back and shook his fist in the air, then tripped over the small table near the top of the steps and flailed wildly. "Whoa…whoa."

Damian stopped at the bottom of the steps and turned with his hands on his hips. Solid thuds were interspersed with Max's pained grunts as the trainee thumped all the way to the bottom and rolled onto the hardwood floors. He groaned and held the top of his head, staring up at the ceiling. Damian gave him a quick once-over, relieved to see no blood or protruding bones.

He looked at him and shook his head. "I'd have to say, you're doing much better at exorcising than hand-to-hand combat. That's a compliment. Trust me. If the opposite were true, you'd be missing a limb or two."

Max opened his eyes and moaned pitifully. His mentor smiled widely and tapped him in the side with his boot. "Come on, slacker. Let's go. We got tapas to eat and coffee to drink."

Damian walked away, and the young priest stared up at the rafters, willing his head to cease pounding in his skull. It didn't help that Astaroth was having a field day with the entire situation. *That was the funniest thing I have ever seen in my life, the way you hung from that mannequin. The only thing that would have made it better is if it pulled your shorts down.*

Max stood belligerently. *I'm glad you find this hilarious. You just went silent. Thanks for that.*

The demon was still laughing. *What could I do? I figured it would be best to hide. This, though? The tumble down the stairs like an old lady? It was fucking priceless. We need to film you.*

CHAPTER TWENTY-FOUR

The night sky sparkled with stars, and the moon was full and bright. Damian had purchased a portable firepit and set it up in the alley near the garage. He dragged a chair around from the courtyard, sat, and tipped his head back to gaze at the heavens. In his lap, his hands gripped the letters from Lucifer and Pandora tightly. It was no secret that Katie had a demon inside her. The whole world knew that, but it wasn't in their face, so the good deeds she did outweighed the bad.

The information in these letters could be devastating if it were to become public knowledge. For them to know she'd aligned herself—even inadvertently through Pandora's history—with the very being they blamed for thousands upon thousands of deaths would start a witch-hunt. Knowing it and seeing it firsthand were two completely different things, especially for people who didn't understand what it was like to be infected. Damian knew that Pandora was not the woman who had once been married to Lucifer. He knew that she had changed—or changed back, whatever the case might be. She had aligned with the right side, and that was what mattered most. She saved lives on a regular basis and made sure to help Katie out of tough situations.

Damian looked at the letters and accepted that he owed Pandora. She had saved his life—or helped Katie do so—on multiple occasions. He couldn't possibly find it in himself to betray her trust and leave something that delicate out in the world for anyone to find. It was a difficult decision because it meant he kept one person's trust while betraying that of an entire religious institution. They might never know about it, but he would.

He leaned forward and opened the letters, then read each one again carefully, committing it to memory. They contained nothing that would help anyone defeat the demons in the war. The only thing they could be used for was to slander Pandora, and ultimately Katie. As he held Lucifer's letter in his hand, he looked at the ink. It shimmered like glitter in the light of the fire. He wondered if it had been written in his own blood imprinted into the skin of a human victim. He read Pandora's letter one last time and tried to imagine her sitting somewhere on Earth while writing it.

The words held a suggestion of her, but nothing close to what she had become. Instead, it read like a woman who had found her freedom and ran from a relationship that had driven her into the ground. It was a letter that he imagined thousands of women across time had written to a man in their life, women who were strong and valiant and able to break free of the chains of an oppressive man. It was a testament to the strength of her gender, showing that suppression could be broken even between two of the most powerful beings alive…or dead.

Whichever way he looked at the letters, they were incredibly intimate. It was a matter between the two of them, and more than that, Pandora's legacy. It was something he felt that even he shouldn't have had the privilege of reading. He knew that if *he* felt that way, no one else on Earth, above in heaven, or below in hell should have the right to read them either. He hoped that one day if someone found his journal, they would feel the same way and keep it hidden.

Damian sighed and folded each of the letters carefully and meticulously into small squares. He looked at the stars and exhaled a deep breath that puffed out as a small cloud. He knew exactly what he needed to do and groaned as he grabbed the fire poker. The heat washed over him as he stoked the blaze and stared into the dancing flames. He listened to the sing-song crackle of the wood, and small sparks floated toward the sky.

When the fire reached its zenith, he tossed the letters into the grate. He watched as Pandora's missive curled slowly and the corners caught fire. Flames consumed it until it dissipated among the coals. Lucifer's letter bathed itself in shimmering blue and red light. It crackled as it unfurled, growing brighter, and finally erupted into ash— just as the demons did when they exorcised them.

Damian nodded, glad he had found the letters. He knew that one day he'd tell Pandora he'd found them, although even Katie wouldn't hear about it. He figured that after everything they had been through and everything that lay ahead, he owed the demon. She was an unexpected ally in the war of the Damned. Hers was the hand that had helped them win against the tyranny of Moloch and his beasts. If no one else in her entire existence had shown her kindness, he would make sure he did.

He sat once more, smiling to himself for a moment. Ravi cleared her throat. *That was a good thing you did.*

The priest didn't respond, but he didn't need to. He grabbed the cardinal's journal, something he had no intention of setting aflame. He turned to the next page and paused. Oddly, several symbols were scribbled across the top of the pages. The handwriting was erratic, and the sentences seemed sporadic, short bursts instead of his normal paragraph form.

January 13, 1966

A day of reckoning has come to me. The truth does not set me free.

On 3 June 1963, the world saw the death of our dear Pope John XXII. He was a kind man with a good heart. No questions were asked.

Just yesterday at the meeting of the Kings, something no one knows about. Revelations. Oh, so many revelations. Pope John was murdered. His death was at the hands of...oh, Lord, save me. I know the truth.

They are rising, and fast. They will find me if I do not go. I know the secrets. I must get away, but where will I go? They know all and see most.

They will attack the Vatican again, just as with Pope John. They will kill, and blood will flow through the halls of the holiest place on Earth. I must get away.

I must cloak in this darkness and go to the place where the

leaves fall twice. There, I will find the answer to my sanctuary.
God keep me safe. They are everywhere. The red is coming.

Until next time.

Damian scowled and read the passage over and over. It was written sloppily and almost frantically. He could almost feel the cardinal's fear through the strokes of his pen, a scary reality and even more so since the passage talked of the death of a Pope at the hand of a demon. The Catholic church had always maintained silence regarding the wars. How could they do that if one of their own had been murdered? There had been no record in anything he had read in the past about an attack on the Vatican.

The priest closed the book and stood, no longer feeling the familiar comfort under the stars. The cardinal had once walked beneath the same ones with fear pulsing through his veins. The man had secrets that only he knew, and it was disconcerting. Damian grabbed the bucket of water beside him and poured it slowly over the flames. Steam rose high, and he stared at the billowing smoke and wondered where the missing man might be at that exact moment. Was he even alive? He had not disappeared before, at least not for a long period of time. Whatever made him run off or had killed him had to be worse than the assassination of a Pope.

Damian glanced at the journal in his hand, tempted to stop reading. He wasn't even halfway through the first, and things already looked bleaker and bleaker with every entry. The writings now made him privy to secrets that he was not supposed to know, and that put him in grave danger. He was suddenly glad that neither Max or Wally knew anything of the contents and that the mystery would remain unsolved for the foreseeable future. With the number of twists and turns in this man's life, it would take Damian a long time to find him. Whatever he did, though, he knew he had to keep those journals secret. It was possible that the future of the church and the life of the cardinal hung in the balance.

He shook his head as he headed for the door. This new adventure had become way bigger than he'd imagined. If nothing else, he wouldn't be bored for a very long time.

The door to the house closed, and Damian locked it behind him. The smoke from the firepit still simmered and billowed upward toward the bright full moon. A few embers in the grate shimmered red and yellow as the ashes cooled. A cold breeze blew through the alley, shifting the smoke toward the fence on the other side of the walk.

From the shadows, a figure stepped forward and through the puffing smoke. His feet barely touched the ground, and he wore a hooded cloak. As he stepped into the light, he pushed the hood down, revealing his long, flowing silver hair. Beneath his cloak, he wore draperies of gold and white adorned with silver thread. His face was kind, and his ice-blue eyes shimmered brightly.

Gabriel walked serenely to the firepit and removed the once again-fully-intact letters. He read them quickly and glanced at the door through which Damian had just passed, and a smile touched his lips. *You have done well, Damian. Your journey will be filled with danger, but you will forever be shrouded by the light of God. May peace find you in your dreams.*

The angel tossed the letters into the firepit and watched as they instantly burst into flames once more and fell to dust among the embers. His eyes flashed a brighter blue as he pulled his hood up and disappeared into the shadows.

AUTHOR NOTES - MICHAEL ANDERLE

WRITTEN NOVEMBER 13, 2018

THANK YOU for not only reading this story but these *Author Notes* as well .

(I think I've been good with always opening with "thank you." If not, I need to edit the other *Author Notes!*)

RANDOM (*sometimes*) THOUGHTS?

So, I've been in talks (it feels like negotiations) with the JIT (Just In Time) team about this series.

I feel like the general thought among readers is that Damian (on his own) is not a fun character. He doesn't have the humor of Pandora and Katie arguing or Ella's snarkiness going for him.

In short, he is kinda dark and dreary at times. We worked to liven things up with his sidekick and the lady across the street trying to kill him with pies, but in general, the stories haven't clicked.

So, we were planning on closing things down until the JIT started asking "where is book 04?"

Well, we have to do a book 04 for closure (we didn't get that totally right), so we WILL have a book 04.

But, we could use some feedback on what YOU think of the series, and what might have gone right and gone wrong with it.

Love to hear your comments – send them to support@lmbpn.com, please

HOW TO MARKET FOR BOOKS YOU LOVE

We are able to support our efforts with you reading our books, and we appreciate you doing this!

If you enjoyed this or ANY book by any author, especially Indie-published, we always appreciate if you make the time to review a book, since it lets other readers who might be on the fence to take a chance on it as well.

AROUND THE WORLD IN 80 DAYS

One of the interesting (at least to me) aspects of my life is the ability to work from anywhere and at any time. In the future, I hope to re-read my own *Author Notes* and remember my life as a diary entry.

So (*for future Mike*) I am sitting in Javier's (a Mexican food restaurant that is a bit expensive but delicious) inside the Aria Casino - second booth on the right - in the bar working on advertising for our Kurtherian Gambit Series, Dark Messiah series, Mr. Brownstone (Go Oriceran!) Series and the Animus series.

The next Mr. Brownstone comes out Friday, and we just confirmed the second cover for the new Alison Brownstone series (got to get those things done ahead of time if possible!)

Next week is Thanksgiving for those here in the US, so I wish you ALL an excellent and safe week. I will be in Los Angeles with family (two of our sons are joining us as well as my older brother and Mom.)

Wherever you are, and whatever you are doing I hope you have a great week!

FAN PRICING

If you would like to find out what LMBPN is doing and the books we will be publishing, just sign up at http://lmbpn.com/email/. When you sign up, we notify you of books coming out for the week, any new posts of interest in the books and pop culture arena, and the fan pricing on Saturday.

Ad Aeternitatem,
Michael Anderle

AUTHOR NOTES - LAURIE STARKEY

OCTOBER 16, 2018

Hey! Hey! Hey!

I know. Kool-Aid Kooler mixed with Fat Albert, but it makes me smile all the same. How are ya?! Firstly, thank you so much for picking up me and Mike's book. We are beyond appreciative of you spending your hard-earned dollars on our form of entertainment.

We both hope you loved the book.

These series and spin-offs have been one of the best parts of 2018 in terms of good literary fun. Nothing like creating a world (even a *damned* one) that you can disappear into and have some adventure with. That's exactly what Damian has been for me at least.

And Ella is getting her debut later this month or early next month, I believe. Anyone need a punk-ass teenager turned bad-ass fighting machine in their lives?

I do, and Melneck, her trusty internal struggle (demon) has been more fun to work with than I should mention. The series has been a joy altogether.

In other news, we're up in freezing cold Massachusetts right now. We did a whirlwind tour this last few weeks. Vegas to see Mike and hang out at his 20Booksto50K event, then Jersey to see Tony Robbins and do one of his events with a group of my staff, and now Massachusetts.

I wanted to come see Boston before heading back to Texas for the holidays, but it is raining like crazy and SO COLD. The Freedom Trail might have to keep on being free without me! Ha!

We're loving life, though. I hope you are, too. Once again, thank you for spending your time with us. We do what we do because of readers like you.

To more stories, because knowing Anderle... there are lots more coming.

Slave to many stories,
Laurie Starkey

PROTECTED BY THE DAMNED

Torn Asunder (1)

Killing Is My Business (2)

And Business Is Good (3)

Sit Down, Shut Up, And Pull The Trigger (4)

Welcome To The Jungle (5)

Metal Up Your Ass (6)

Dirty Deeds Done Dirt Cheap (7)

For Whom The Bell Tolls (8)

WAR OF THE DAMNED

Resurrection Of The Damned (1)

No Quarter (2)

Dark Is The Night (3)

Dim Glows The Horizon (4)

Waking The Leviathan (5)

Subversive Giants (6)

Juntto (7)

DAMIAN'S CHRONICLES

Crucifix (1)

Renegade (2)

Apostle (3)

www.ingramcontent.com/pod-product-compliance
Lightning Source LLC
Chambersburg PA
CBHW050253110726
47898CB00007B/2391